THE REDEMPTION OF THE CANNIBAL WOMAN

THE REDEMPTION OF THE CANNIBAL WOMAN

AND OTHER STORIES

Marco Denevi

Translated by Alberto Manguel

COACH HOUSE PRESS
TORONTO

Coach House Press
50 Prince Arthur Avenue, Suite 107
Toronto, Canada M5R 1B5

Published with the assistance of the Department
of Communications, the Ontario Arts Council
and the Ontario Publishing Centre.

Editor for the Press: Alberto Manguel
Cover Design: Shari Spier / Reactor
Cover Photograph: *Deux Sailors, 1989* by Steven Jack
Printed in Canada

Canadian Cataloguing in Publication Data
Denevi, Marco, 1922–
    The redemption of the cannibal woman and other stories
ISBN 0-88910-443-3
I. Title.
PQ7797.D394R43 1993   863   C93-093448-2

CONTENTS

MICHEL

Hey, come on, of course my name is not Michel. My name is Gonzalo Maritti. I'll never know why the old lady—her name was Rosina Maritti, Italian—gave me that Spanish name, Gonzalo. But at Le Matelot all the waiters had to have French names. One of the funny ideas of the boss, Gaston, whose real name was Hector. It was Freddy who chose Michel, because I, to tell you the truth, don't know a fucking word of French. I had been working at Le Matelot for a week. It was my first job, you know, because while the old lady was alive she supported me so that I could go to school. I didn't really go to school, but I wanted to keep the old lady happy, so I would tell her I did. So when the old lady died I found myself out on the street. Freddy, who knows everyone from God upwards, found me the job at the bar. He was a friend of Gaston and Gaston, as soon as he saw me, looked at Freddy and said yes, I'd be okay.

No kidding, I'd be okay. Eighteen years old and so handsome it made you do a double take. Now you see me sort of worn out, but just imagine me then. Two days later I was the most popular of the waiters. Gaston first sent me to the tables, but then saw the looks I was getting and stood me behind the bar. You should have seen the fruits at the bar. They would shake my hand, try to chat me up, ask me for a match every five minutes. But I stayed on my perch. Polite, sure, but on my perch. Because, after all, who were they, the whole fucking lot? Snotty kids like myself. That was the worst about Le Matelot. It was full of kids. And what was I going to do with kids, you tell me. I was expecting something else, you understand. Something like Freddy, when Freddy was loaded and, say, three years younger. But Freddy was now broke and he had suddenly turned into a little old man, with one foot in the grave, because of his illness, you know.

The night the guy appeared, the whole lot of fruits at the bar stopped cackling, imagine that, and nailed him on the spot with their eyes. Then they started elbowing each other and ruffling their feathers. Or as Gaston would say, took out their powder-puffs. Look *who* was making fun of the fruits! But the guy wasn't looking at any of them. He looked at me, you know, from the very first moment.

The guy was sort of forty years old, shaped like a body-builder, blond, bronzed. He looked like Buster Crabbe, to give you an idea. You don't know who he is. It doesn't matter. He was a guy who played Tarzan when you weren't yet born. In my room I had a photo of Buster Crabbe—Freddy had bought it for me—dressed in a tiger-skin loincloth, patting a lion, and smiling like a toothpaste ad. A guy like that, yes, I thought. I would even have done it like for free. Well maybe not completely free. But it would be enough if he just took me to dinner or bought me a tie. But to tell you the truth, what I'd really have liked was if he'd made me his bodyguard or his private secretary. During the day, everything above-board. And at night ... you understand. Or that he'd adopt me as his son. Can you imagine? Who would know? And I'd be okay in the bucks department.

I swooped down on him like an eagle. Watch my tactics. I put both hands on the edge of the counter, lean forward towards the customer, and in a low voice, serious, you know, but polite, I ask him: 'Can I get you something, sir?' Because there are assholes who say 'What you having?' But where do they think they are? In a donut shop? I instead would ask: 'Can I get you something, sir?' Notice the difference? I get *you* something. I to *you*. Because that's why I'm here, to serve you, and you are here to order. You ask and I obey. Customers with class can appreciate these things. They notice them just like that and they thank you for them. He answered: 'A J&B.' Terrific, I thought. He's not one of those misers who asks for orange juice or local booze.

He had a butch voice and a face that, seen close up,

was unbelievable, I swear. And the clothes! Italian tie, poplin shirt, a light-grey three-piece made in heaven. I used to be crazy about clothes, and figured out how much the lot was worth.

I was still leaning towards him. 'Ice? Water? Perrier?'

'On the rocks.'

'Yes, sir.'

And all the while I stared into his eyes, green eyes, so green they sent a shiver down your back, know what I mean, and he also was staring. Both very serious, you understand. No cutesy smiles. But the kind of serious ... I don't know how to explain ... the kind of serious of two guys passing some secret information they don't want others to find out.

I was about to get the whisky when I saw him put a cigarette to his mouth. In a flash I lit it with my solid-gold Dupont. Freddy had given me the Dupont. It always worked and in the darkness of the place it shone like a jewel. He thanked me with a nod and kept looking. There was something already, just a little, but already something between the two of us.

Now came a bit of just being the bartender. I went up to the shelves, got the bottle of J&B, the glass, the pail of ice, the measuring cup, asked Gaston for the bill, all this without looking at him, almost always turning my back on him, but everything very fast, you know, to see if he'd still watch, to show him that I knew that he was a classy customer and that you mustn't make classy customers wait.

I came back and poured out the J&B in front of him, something I didn't do for everyone, even if they asked for the real stuff, and said: 'One? Two?'

'Two, please.'

I put in the two ice cubes, mark the bill, and now to the third part of my tactics. You stand very close to the customer, very straight, not looking at him, and you watch the tables or the people in the street. But if the guy pulls out another cigarette you run to light it. So the guy realizes that even if you're looking somewhere else you're really watching him, and if you're not looking at him straight in the eye it's so as not to get on his tits and to let him drink in peace, but that you are there, near enough, ready to satisfy his every wish. You know, a classy customer appreciates these things.

The nuisance was the fruits at the bar, all ruffled up as they were, wanting to spoil my game. They were trying to draw the guy's attention and they found nothing better than calling me at the top of their voice:

'Michel, another glass of water.'

'Michel, another daiquiri.'

'Michel, a light.'

And Michel this and Michel that. Well, anyway, at least he'd know my name. He could see that the customers were friendly with me and that even if they tried to be a bit too friendly I was able to handle it without going too far, you understand. That if I wasn't an easy pick-up, I wasn't an untouchable, either.

The guy, from time to time, looked around the place. The fruits, thinking that he wanted to make connections, would get all frantic. But he would look at me again or look into his glass, and smoke. I noticed everything without having to pin my eyes on him, and was having a laugh all to myself. The kids also realized what was happening, because they have experience, you know. But no one said anything to me. That's a sacred law in this world, you know. Had I been on the other side of the bar, then yes, one would have come up to me and said: 'Congratulations, darling. It seems you hooked yourself a beauty.'

But I was just a waiter, and they would not give in. And out of spite, just to break my balls, they kept asking for this and asking for that. Break *my* balls. Poor darlings.

Just as one of the fruits at the bar, I don't remember which one, was making me change his glass, I saw that Jorge, better known as Jorgelina, a fag who was into drugs and threw wild parties at his house, or so they say because I never went to one, was pouring half a glass of rum and Coke on Buster Crabbe's sleeve just to get to talk to him.

I left the guy who wanted his glass changed and ran

to the other end of the bar, where Buster Crabbe was sitting. Just to show him that for me, he was more important than that whole bunch of fags put together.

Jorge, with that voice of his, like a pregnant chicken, said: 'Oh I'm so sorry, so sorry,' and pulled out a handkerchief and tried to mop the sleeve. Buster Crabbe, without even looking at what the other was doing, answered: 'It's okay,' and went on drinking his whisky.

When I came up to him, it seemed to me that he was smiling with his eyes, you know, like saying to me: 'But can you imagine how far a fruit like this will go?' I stood there very formal, you know, not wanting to make Jorgelina angry, after all she leaves me three big ones every night, and said: 'Allow me, sir.'

And I also pulled out my handkerchief, the only one left of the lot Freddy had given me, Irish linen, real class.

He stopped me: 'Don't bother, thanks.' But you see, not aggressively. You know, I say aggressively, and my head fills up with things I remember. *Aggressively*. That was Freddy's favourite word. For Freddy you were or you were not aggressive, somebody loved aggressively or made fun of you aggressively. I know what he meant. For example, Buster Crabbe said 'don't bother.' And he said it seriously, but not aggressively. On the contrary. Look, it was like he was being serious just to show me that there, among the bunch of kids, the only one of his own kind was me, but that he didn't or couldn't show it in front of everyone, so he would show it just a little, in a way that no one would know, so that only I, so intelligent, would know. And to tell you the truth, I liked that. And I decided to carry on with his little game.

So that when, after the 'don't bother' he asked me for another drink I said very seriously and without looking at him: 'Yes, sir.' And I went off to get the J&B.

I heard Jorge's clucking: 'Am I forgiven?' And the butch voice of Buster Crabbe: 'Yes, if you buzz off.'

Incredible! That guy was incredible! I was dying to laugh, really. I wanted to turn around and see the look on the fruit's face. But when I got to the bar and managed to turn around, Jorge had disappeared and Buster Crabbe was smoking another cigarette and I had lost my chance to light it and, maybe, start a conversation.

He stayed there all night. From time to time he would check out the kids at the bar or the couples on the dancefloor, but with a self-sufficient look, you know, like the guy who knows what he's doing. Not like those greaseballs who sometimes appeared at Le Matelot by chance, and when they realized where they were, they'd pull a face that you knew meant they wanted to start bashing up the fruits. Not him, you see? He watched them as if it were a show, just for the fun of it. But at about two o'clock he began to look bored. Of course: he wanted the whole bunch of fruits to fuck off and leave him alone with me, so that we could talk in peace and quiet. Because an English gentleman like that wasn't going to open up in front of that birdcage. But one thing was certain: he kept looking at me, more and more. This is what he'd do: he would stare me in the eye, then look away, then stare again, then look away again, and it went on like that for hours. Just like Freddy, when Freddy met me at La Farola. I was sure he was getting ready for the big move.

I too wanted everyone to leave. But they wouldn't. When two would leave, three would come in, and the bar would be again full of people. I thought it was about time to make him understand that I knew what he wanted and that I was with him all the way, because I was afraid that this guy would get fed up with sitting and waiting, and take off. So I started smiling. But listen: I've got my tactics. Freddy always said that I was the only one he knew who could smile without stretching his lips. He said I was a ventriloquist with smiles. Buster Crabbe understood as quickly as that; I knew, because his eyes began to sparkle.

I helped him to his third drink without asking Gaston.

'This one's on the house, sir.'

I poured the whisky for him and put in the two ice cubes, and it seemed to me that knowing that he wanted it on the rocks, to help him to it without asking, was like knowing all his tastes, like being his private secretary, his right arm. It was great.

And just as I was about to go and place myself, as I said before, just a few steps away from him, he said in a low voice: 'Thanks, Michel.'

It sent shivers all down my spine. You see? He had called me Michel. A guy who had come to Le Matelot for the first time, a fancy guy, an English gentleman, and with those great looks ... No problem, Buster Crabbe was mine.

But then, so that no one would catch on to what was happening, I started to look serious. Well, to tell you the truth, a little because I didn't want anybody to notice, and also because, when one of those guys tries to pick me up, I don't know why, I just get angry and nervous. The same happened with Freddy. You should have seen what Freddy looked like when I met him. I was barely fifteen. Well, who remembers Freddy now? The thing is that if you had come into Le Matelot that night and seen me, you would have thought that I was mad as hell.

At last, at almost half-past four, he was the only one at the bar and there was just one couple left necking on the dancefloor.

Then I saw, even though I was pretending to look somewhere else, that he was calling me with his hand. I ran up to him. Again I put both hands on the bar, leaned forward towards him, like the first time—remember I told you what my tactics were—but now I looked him in the eye and smiled at him with my whole face. In the early morning I always looked more handsome. I looked pale, with dark-blue lines under my eyes, and everybody said I was the spitting image of James Dean. On many nights, around that time, one of the customers, pissed as hell, would ask, in a hoarse voice: 'Michel, Michel, how much do you charge?'

But all he said was: 'Last one,' and pointed at the glass.

I served him his fourth J&B. The bill was twelve hundred pesos. I just stood next to him, in front of him, not trying to hide anything, as if waiting, as if giving him rope. He looked at me and smiled, a little pissed, I thought. When they're pissed even the straightest guys kick their shoes off. Then, in a low voice, I don't know why, because Gaston was at the other end of the bar adding up his figures, and the couple was necking about thirty feet away, but maybe to make the conversation more intimate, or maybe because he wanted the whole thing to be mysterious, he asked: 'Is your name really Michel?' He asked it outright, the bastard. And suddenly I thought: a cop. Again I pretended to look sad, but what I was was angry and frightened.

'No sir. They make you change your name here.'

'And what is your real name?'

'Gonzalo.'

He lowered his eyes and sent me a Colgate smile. 'Nice name. I like it better than Michel.'

'I do too, sir.'

That's true. Michel sounds like a fruit. Michel is okay for a hairdresser or for a dressmaker, but not for me. Gonzalo is a nice butch name, Spanish but butch.

He drank down the whisky as if he were dying of thirst, as if it were Pepsi. I, still thinking he was a cop, looked towards the street, but just in case I looked angry.

'Have you been working here long?'

'One week.'

'And do you like this job?'

Nice trap. Who did he think I was? Like born yesterday?

'No, sir. I don't really like it.'

'And why do you do it then?'

'Beggars can't be choosers. I couldn't get anything better.'

'How old are you?'

'Eighteen, almost nineteen.'

'And your parents don't mind?'

We spoke as if we were at confession. I know it looked as if we were making some strange deal. Gaston, from the other end, had realized that something was happening as he told me afterwards. But if you couldn't hear us, you would have thought that I was like squealing to the cops, because I was answering so aggressively. See, Freddy's word. It's stuck, since the old days, and I still use it. Well, as I was saying, I was answering aggressively. But he kept asking ever so nicely.

'I have no parents, sir. I have no one. I'm alone in the world.' I said it all at once. If he was with the police, that would be useful. To be an orphan, to be eighteen, to be alone in the world ...

He sat there a while in silence. A long while, so long, that I at last dared to look at him. His eyes were shining. What eyes, dear God! As if he had been sniffing coke. He was even better-looking than Buster Crabbe.

To hide those eyes, the eyes of a tiger, he looked down again. 'Where do you live?'

'Canning and Las Heras.'

'Alone?'

For the cops, living alone is a point against you. But maybe he was asking to see whether I had a place for us to go. In any case, with Mrs. Zulma, I couldn't take the risk. So, I thought, the best thing is to tell him the truth.

'No. I have a place in a rooming-house. I used to live there with my mother. But since my mother died ....'

'Long ago?'

'Ten days.'

'Oh, I'm sorry.'

Sure he was sorry. He was just pretending, good manners and all that, but inside, I thought, he's dancing on one leg.

I, just in case he was a cop, even though he didn't really look like a cop, kept on explaining. 'Before we had two rooms, Mum and I. But now with one it's enough.'

'I understand.'

'I had to tighten the old belt.'

'I understand. Of course.'

He was silent for a while, looking at the glass and turning it in his hands. There was no whisky left in it. Only half a melted ice cube. I was waiting. I knew, because of Freddy, that a guy who's young, good-looking and broke is the best bait.

'Michel.'

'Yes, sir?'

He was still silent, looking at the glass. He preferred Gonzalo but he still called me Michel. He didn't dare stop pretending. He was even shyer than Freddy. Or maybe more of a gentleman. And I was looking at him desperately, wanting to say to him: But yes, my love, I understand and I'm here, I'm all yours. I'll be your bodyguard, I thought. I'll be your adopted son. To call you Dad in front of everyone and even kiss you, without anyone saying anything, and at night be your lover and still call you Dad. That was always my dream. But Freddy didn't want to be called Dad.

Finally he said it. 'Michel, what time do you leave?'

'We close at five. Quarter past I'm out.'

He had begun the final run. I swear my heart was beating, because of all the emotion and also because I was frightened he might be a cop. A gay cop would have been okay. A cop, someone in the army, maybe an airline pilot, thinking of me for some fun. Another of my fantasies.

Suddenly he nailed me on the spot with his eyes. I understood why. Because if he had asked me while he was looking down it would have seemed as if he were begging for something, something he was ashamed of, but he had to make me believe that he wasn't asking for anything dirty, and that he wasn't offending me, wasn't frightening me, you understand?

'Michel, I'll wait for you outside in my car. It's parked at the corner of Libertador. It's a black Thunderbird.'

A cop doesn't have a black Thunderbird. Even if he is into all sorts of funny business. A cop doesn't spend all night drinking whisky. What for? To know if Le Matelot is what everybody knows it is, even the lollipop ladies, even Mrs. Zulma? To lay a trap for me? Me? And who was I? Was I Al Capone to spend all that effort on me? No. All this song and dance was not stuff for a cop. This was more along Freddy's line, someone more careful than Freddy.

So quietly, just like that, I said: 'I'll be there at a quarter past five.'

That way, if he had felt embarrassed, I'd show him there was no need.

He paid, left me an enormous tip that I pocketed without a word, and he left without saying goodbye. You see, I liked the fact that he didn't say goodbye. It was a way of saying, I'll be waiting.

Gaston asked: 'So, who was that guy?'

'What guy?'

'The guy who just left.'

I looked towards the door as if I didn't quite remember. 'Sort of blond ...?'

'Yeah, that one.'

'I think he was a cop.'

'Why?'

'He was asking things.'

'What things?'

'If I had seen a fat gay guy around here, white hair, someone called Rudi.'

'Not here.'

'That's what I said.'

'And he didn't tell you why he was looking for him?'

'You crazy? Why would he tell me?'

'So why do you think he's a cop?'

'I don't know. I just thought so.'

'No, he's no cop.'

Quarter past five I was at the corner of Libertador, next to the black Thunderbird, red seats, a dream. I felt like really cool. I had looked at myself in the cloakroom mirror and, let me tell you, seeing myself in a mirror made me feel good. Because with a face like that I had a right to everything. To pick up Buster Crabbe the very first night at Le Matelot, I, the bartender, and not the fruits at the bar with their Rolexes on their wrists and their Peugeots at the door. The right to get Buster Crabbe to buy me suits, shirts, ties, let me drive his Thunderbird, and maybe one day take me with him to Europe, and there in Europe, who knows, I might pick someone up with even more bucks.

First we just talked any old shit. That the car's brakes were not working well, that it cost him an arm and a leg to keep it, and that he wanted to change it for a domestic make. I remember that the same thing happened with Freddy. You know why? Because at first they feel a little over-excited, a little too uneasy. You know, it's all a bit too quick, so just talking like that, talking about just anything, like two friends, like two straight guys, the situation becomes easier. Or maybe, who knows, they are so happy they can't believe it, and they try to go into it slowly just to get accustomed, not to get too nervous, or to convince themselves they're not dreaming, as they must have dreamt so many times of some young guy who escapes with some skirt, and here they had me, in the car, next to them, ready for anything, I, with my face and my body.

But three minutes later, without looking at me, staring out of the window in front of him, he asked: 'And before working in the bar, what did you do?'

'I went to school.'

'And what did you live on?'

I didn't have to lie. 'My mother earned enough for both of us.'

'What did you study?'

This is where I had to make up something.

'Technical school.'

'Probably the last year, I imagine.'

'The last year. And that's when I had to leave.'

'What would you have liked to be?'

'An engineer.'

'A good profession.'

Look, you have to let them ask you everything, about your family, about the dog, about the neighbour's parrot. Because a friend already knows all that and doesn't need to ask you anything. But they, just think of it, they don't know you at all. So you have to give them a speed course because if you don't, they have to go to bed with you like cold and they don't like that, they don't trust it, they think they're just going to bed with some fucking sailor, and little English gentlemen like Freddy don't enjoy that.

'Couldn't you find another job? Because look I'm sorry to say so, but Le Matelot is a terrible place.'

It made me a little angry, this putting on airs. So I said to him: 'So what were you doing there?' I said it so aggressively that I felt sorry and changed my tune: 'I mean, is that the first time you've been there?'

'First and last.'

'And how did you find it?'

'By chance. I don't live in Buenos Aires. I live away most of the year.'

'In Europe?'

'No, in the country. In Córdoba.'

I let out a little laugh, loud enough for him to hear me.

'What are you laughing at?'

'Nothing. You know what I thought you were? A cop.'

He also laughed, but louder. 'What made you think I was a cop?'

'I don't know. The things you asked.'

'Did they bother you?'

'No.'

'Have you had trouble with the police?'

'No. What trouble?'

'But you're afraid of them.'

'No, never. Why should I be afraid? But Le Matelot has a bad reputation, so even if I'm clean I can get hit on the rebound.'

We had reached that little square at the end of Avenida Alvear. He stopped the car. He turned around, his whole body, and looked me in the eye. I sat sideways, against the door, and also looked at him. The moment has come, I thought.

'Do you usually accept invitations from customers at the bar?'

You can imagine, I didn't like that. But I knew that Buster Crabbe was really like Freddy. Freddy went to the same places, liked the same things, did the same stuff as the other gays, but didn't want to be mistaken for one of them. You've got to see the difference, he used to say. The difference of what? The difference between a fruit like Jorge who says it to you in the face as soon as she sees you, and these here, who instead talk to you first about the brakes of the car not working? But okay, just humour them. Anyway, I like them like that. Something else I'll tell you: Freddy used to go to all sorts of gay bars, was always surrounded by young kids and fruits, and then he'd be all worried because everyone would say he was gay. I'll never understand that.

I answered, without seeming offended: 'This is the first time.'

'And why did you accept this time?'

'Because I know the difference.'

Freddy would have liked the flattery. But he didn't seem to. He was more complicated than Freddy.

'But you thought I was a cop.'

'All the braver, then, for accepting.'

Dig that one, I thought. He couldn't help smiling. 'So this sort of place didn't corrupt you?'

I was beginning to understand. He liked first nights. But I played dumb: 'Corrupt how?'

'I don't know. I imagine that at Le Matelot there must be drug addicts, car thieves, hustlers ...'

I was waiting for the word. And he said it: '... homosexuals.'

I had on my best innocent face. 'I don't think so. They all seem like guys from good families.'

'But you yourself said that Le Matelot had a bad reputation.'

I'd been an asshole. I tried to fix it up. 'Yes, like all the bars around here. People talk, but ...'

'Not all the bars have a bad reputation.'

'But you saw, there were lots of straight couples.'

'I mean the ones at the bar.'

'If those are homosexuals, then I don't know. I only know them as customers at the bar. And all they do there is have a drink and talk.'

'Talk to you.'

'So who talks to me? All they say is, give me a whisky, give me a light, give me the bill, and that's all.'

'That's all?'

I was starting to get angry. I looked at him: 'What else?'

27

'Ask you to go out with them.'

'Never.'

'So I'm the first. Of course you've been working there for barely a week. They're probably waiting to know you better.'

The bastard was making fun of me, and how. I was getting really mad. 'Yes, sir. The first. The first even if I had been working there for ten years.'

He also seemed angry: 'And to what do I owe the honour of having been accepted?'

I got aggressive: 'I told you. Because I know how to distinguish. And I thought you also knew how to distinguish. But I was wrong, so I'm sorry.' I thought: here he gets really mad. But no, he laughed.

'Don't get angry. I'm not asking these questions with any bad intention. But don't you think it's a little strange to go out with a man the first time you see him?'

I shrank back in my seat, looked out in front of me, spoke as if I had a knot in my throat. 'Very, very strange, yeah. Except if you're alone in the world and have no parents, no friends, no one. The only people you know are these nicely brought-up kinds who treat you as if you were their servant. So it's not so strange if you catch on to the first rope somebody throws you. Some sort of feeling, some affection. Something to make you feel like a person, not just a bartender.'

I turned around and looked him in the eye, ready to

go for it. I know how to make tears come to my eyes. 'But if I was wrong about you, or you were wrong about me, I can get out here, and walk back home.' I thought: either he beats me up or he kisses me.

He didn't do either. He looked at me for a long while, with a really strange face, like studying me. This one is really weirder than Freddy, I thought. Then he patted my leg, he patted it a little more than necessary (he must have been testing the quality, I thought), and said: 'Okay.'

Nothing more: 'Okay.'

He started the car again, took Cerrito, two blocks further, and stopped the car. He pointed to a door. 'I've got a flat there, where I stay when I come to Buenos Aires. Come up with me.' And, as he thought I had made some sort of gesture (I hadn't moved), he looked at me: 'Come on. Don't be afraid.' Again the Colgate smile: 'I'm not what you think.'

Freddy's very same words. I answered, as I had to Freddy: 'I know, sir.'

Again he sat there for a while studying me (I thought he was thinking: maybe I'm stuck with this goof). Then he said: 'I've got to talk to you.'

The same as Freddy, Freddy, when he took me that first night to his place, had to talk to me. And as soon as we got in he started taking his clothes off.

He opened the door of the car. I got out by the

29

other door. There was no one in the street. We entered the building. No one saw us go in. We crossed a hall almost as big as Le Matelot, all carpeted. At the far end were elevators. We got into one, also carpeted and full of mirrors. I looked up and saw myself so handsome that I understood that Buster Crabbe had been putting up a fight up to the very last minute because he knew that with me he was lost. We got to a certain floor, he opened the door of an apartment, turned on the light, and I was just looking around when he started hugging me.

'Gonzalo,' he said with half a voice, and I thought that he was panting. 'Gonzalo.'

I also began to hug him, but slowly, to make him want me more.

'Gonzalo,' he said, and he held my face with one hand. 'I've got something to say to you.'

'It's not necessary,' I said. 'I know.' And I kissed him on the mouth.

Look, it was all so quick and unexpected that I don't really remember. I know that with both his hands he shook my arms from his body. I saw that his face looked terrible. And immediately he began to beat me up.

You know, I can't stand anybody laying a finger on me. Not even the old lady ever hit me. Least of all one of these guys. So when he began hitting me, a sort of madness came over me. I don't know what I did. All I

30

know is that I saw him lying on the floor, the eyes open, and the blond hair full of blood. I felt his chest. He was dead.

Imagine, I was so frightened I could have shit my pants. I ran from the apartment. At six I was back home.

For a while I couldn't sleep. I thought that nobody had seen me with the guy, so that when they discovered the body, the cops, even if they looked far and wide, would not be able to incriminate me. And if they found out about his visit to Le Matelot, well, so what? I didn't know him, I had served him some drinks till half-past four, then he had left and I hadn't seen him again, and I would also tell them the story I had told Gaston, of the little fat white-haired fruit, a certain Rudi, and Gaston would be my witness, and the police would think it was some sort of a gay crime. I was also thinking, why had he beaten me up? Where had I gone wrong? I thought first that he was maybe one of these loonies who first leads you on and then beats you up, or first beats you up and then gets you into bed. At last I fell asleep and slept till two in the afternoon.

At two o'clock Mrs. Zulma came in. 'Come on, get up,' she shouted. 'What time will you have lunch?'

Look, I'll tell it to you all in one go, because at first I was half-asleep and didn't understand what she was asking and didn't answer, and then, when I began to realize, I got so desperate I almost went crazy.

31

'Listen, didn't a man go to see you, last night, at the bar? Tall blond, very good-looking? Because last night, as soon as you left, he came round here and asked for you. I told him you weren't here, that you had gone out. He wanted to know more, but I, just imagine, didn't know who he was so I wouldn't tell him anything, because I thought, God knows who this one is and probably that good-for-nothing got into some trouble. But when he showed me the envelope with a letter and I recognized your poor mother's handwriting I changed my mind. Yes, I never said anything to you because Rosina asked me not to say anything. But now I will. The day before she died Rosina gave me a sealed envelope with a letter inside, to put in the mailbox after she died. But Rosina, I said to her, you're not going to die. I told her that to make her feel better, because I knew she wasn't going to last more than twenty-four hours. And she also knew it, poor soul. Well, that's how it was. Two or three days after we buried her I put the envelope in the mailbox. It was addressed to a certain Gonzalo of this-and-that, a lot of very distinguished surnames, and the address was an estate in Córdoba. Rosina had asked me not to say anything to you, because if the letter didn't achieve any results you didn't need to know, but obviously it did, and that's why I'm telling you. So when the man showed me the envelope I realized that he was the Gonzalo from Córdoba, and told him everything. He was here for almost an hour, asking about Rosina and about you, especially about you. He wanted to know what you were like, what you did, what you didn't do. I told him that you used to go to school, but that now, after Rosina's death, you had to start to work, as a bartender, and in a place I really didn't like. He told me he'd go there, to meet you. Didn't he go? Maybe he thought better of it and meant to meet you here. And I think he chose well, because that bar, my boy, let me tell you … So get up and get dressed, because he'll probably be here any moment now and you shouldn't keep him waiting. Because you can see he's a gentleman, and the car he has, so luxurious. I bet he hasn't come all the way from Córdoba just to give you his condolences. I don't know a thing, but for some reason Rosina gave you his name. Poor Rosina, always so proud. She probably never told him, but when she knew you were going to be alone in the world she sent him the letter. Get up and get dressed, this is probably your big day.'

Then the bell rang.

'What did I tell you? I bet it's him.'

It was the police. They had reached me through the letter the old lady had sent him and which they found in his pocket. They didn't suspect anything. They were just coming to ask a few questions, that's all. But I immediately confessed.

LETTER TO GIANFRANCO

Dear Gianfranco, on Monday I'm leaving for Paris. Just like that: for Paris and in a plane. It has to be Monday because I've just read in the paper that every Monday at eleven p.m. there's a plane leaving for Paris, and I never get on a plane except at night, at eleven p.m. And why Paris of all places? Why not Paris of all places, is what I say. One ends up going to Paris as if one were going to a wedding or a funeral, whether one is in the mood for it or not, through a quirk of fate. As soon as I arrive, I'll send you a postcard of the Eiffel Tower and a kitsch message: *Dear Gianfranco, I left for Paris on Monday and in Paris my first thoughts are of you.*

I'll stop at a small hotel that appears in a novel by Francis Carco. The hotel is situated in a neighbourhood of ill repute, on a tortuous street paved with rough pink cobblestones, around the corner from a bistro where whores, apaches and bohemians meet. The owner of the hotel is a lady who speaks a little Portuguese. Her name is Madame Pomargue and in her youth she was a show girl, at least that's what she says. This lady won't object to my bringing up to my room the men who will pursue me along the boulevards or offer me a cheap cognac in the bistro. On the contrary, she'll give me a room with strategic mirrors and the red drapes of a bawdy house, she'll lend me her scandalous underwear from the days when she worked at the circus, and she'll teach me the argot of the underworld. In the morning, she'll bring me breakfast in bed and she'll want me to tell her my adventures of the previous night. According to Francis Carco, she's a very agreeable lady but she has a maddening weakness for dwarves. I'll see to it that none of my lovers is a dwarf, otherwise Madame Pomargue might become jealous and look for a way to steal him away from me. I believe her capable of murdering me for the sake of a handsome lilliputian.

I still don't know where I'll find the money for the fare. I'm almost certain I'll climb onto the plane without a ticket, but looking like someone rather fed up with travelling to Paris every Monday night. When up there the inspector comes round asking to see our tickets and I tell him that I've forgotten mine at home, do you think they'll hurl me into the air through one of those little round windows? Will they be as brutish as that to a woman travelling all on her own to Paris, to Madame Pomargue's hotel? I think that instead they'll consider me their guest of honour, offer me champagne and caviar, and when we reach the airport they'll call for the red-carpeted stairway. They will have wired ahead from the plane, and at the airport a crowd of handsome young men will be waiting for me, all specialists in South American women and single female poets, all bearing the names of film stars and the nicknames of pimps and gigolos. But I'll leave on the arm of one as blond as you, tall as you, someone with your eyes, green in the middle and golden around the edge, someone who, like you, loves women like me.

Now I feel very happy. Suddenly I was overcome by this crazy urge to write you a letter, and now I'm writing it. On the radio I heard them say that it had stopped raining and that the sun was shining. All lies, Gianfranco. It's a trap, so that you and I will go out into the streets and drown in some God-forsaken gutter. They want us to die before we meet at our usual place, in the café at the corner of Paraguay and Maipú, so that afterwards the street-sweepers sweep us up like a couple of piles of dry leaves, like a couple of dead rats. It's still raining, Gianfranco. Rain repeats itself, it is always the same rain, like the chorus in an opera. Comes down on one side, rises on the other, comes down again and will continue like this until the rainwater is all worn out. It's not worth watching it. You just stay in your room and I'll stay in mine. In my room I am writing you this letter, in your room you are reading it.

In your room is a wood stove and in the stove a big blazing fire. You are wearing raw-silk pyjamas and over

36

the pyjamas a cerulean-coloured dressing-gown. I have no idea what a cerulean colour looks like, but many times I've read of 'a cerulean-coloured sky,' 'Valentina's cerulean-coloured dress,' and I imagine a colour so beautiful that I have never been able to give it any particular tone. Gianfranco, you're a little dishevelled but it suits you, it lends you an air of adolescence midway between anguish and ardour, indifference and caprice. From where I am I can smell your perfume, that cologne you wear, that scent of blond tobacco, citrus fruit and fine wood, which envelops you as if you yourself were its source, as if you were made not of flesh and bones but of some other substance giving off this fragrance. Because you're not a man like other men, Gianfranco. You don't possess their vulgarity, their libidinous lust. You are not a fetid boar like the rest of them. You are made entirely out of spirit.

Don't go out, you stubborn man. It is not yet midday. It's raining and when it rains all the hours of the day are hours without rendezvous or engagements, they're hours in which to write letters or read them. Nor is it Tuesday today, nor any other day in the week. When it rains it's a day wedged in between two days like a lover between a husband and a wife. Therefore, sit in your armchair by the fire, cross your legs, no, women cross their legs and certain very thin melancholic men, you place your right heel over the left knee, lean back, rest your neck against the top edge of the armchair, and in this position that shows you off as in a floral arrangement, hold in one hand a cigarette and in the the other my letter, and read me, Gianfranco, read me.

There's no heating here. After five days of rain my room has begun to melt and drip like a wax candle. The walls have turned into sponges or moist bread-dough, the furniture is soft and from the ceiling fall slow and bothersome drops. For five whole days I have barely left the bed. My cookies are all gone, as well as the cheese and the coffee, but it doesn't matter because with the dampness the cookies had turned to old felt, the cheese tasted of beauty soap and the coffee of laxative.

These past days I've read nothing but the newspapers. They're all old newspapers, but I don't care. On the contrary, it does me good to read old newspapers. I feel safe from crime, from death and from catastrophes that have reached other people, and I instead read about them in the papers that say that it all happened today, that today a plane crashed, today a fire broke out, today a bomb exploded, today, today, today, and for me it's yesterday or the day before yesterday, and here I am, saved, away from that today that gobbles up the living. Reading old newspapers I feel almost eternal.

I read even the classified ads. What a relief to read them and know that those vacancies are already filled and that I don't need to get up early in order to find a job. Before, I used to read them in the perilous today and would always fall into their trap. 'Well-educated young lady able to type properly,' and I'd be off. But there I'd meet them, the women, so tall, so well-brought-up, so heartless, dressed in the latest fashion, with ochre eyelids and mandarin nails. The first thing they'd do was ask me my age. Sometimes I'd say thirty-eight and sometimes forty-two. A few would arch their thin Greek-chorus eyebrows and protest: 'But the ad specified secretaries under twenty-five.' Others, without looking at me, but with a grimace of disgust as if I were importuning them with my mere presence, would hand me a piece of paper. The paper was a job application. Academic degrees, languages spoken, salary expectations. And references. I would never know what to put under 'references,' so I'd always put your name. Then they'd take the application without reading it, without even looking at me, and staring out of the window or deciphering their Fu Manchu nails, they'd say: 'We'll give you a call, good afternoon.' But they never called to offer me the job. Do you know why, Gianfranco? Because they expected me to read the ads on the next day, and go and apply once again, and once again they'd be able to ask me my age. The whole thing was a trap. Happily, I've since opened my eyes. And what they don't know is that I've deceived them. Because nowhere on the application did I say that in 1961 I received a poetry prize, and that the poet César Tiempo wrote in the magazine *Davar* that my book was like a collection of block-prints (I don't know if he said block-prints or miniatures), illuminated by the hand of the Limbourgs. But they don't know, nor do they know who the Limbourgs were.

The newspapers also print the list of conferences and art exhibits. I used to attend the conferences. But now, at last, I've come to realize that all conferences are a stupid joke played on us by the lecturers. They pretend to be speaking about Ortega y Gasset, or about the problem of the Latin American novel, but in fact they repeat for a full hour nonsensical phrases, mingling without rhyme or reason paragraphs taken from literary textbooks. All conferences are the same conference, but the lecturers change the order of the words and pronounce them as if they were convinced of what they were saying, and they even accompany the whole thing with gestures. And the foolish public sit there listening and understand nothing but look as if they understood and finally break into applause and think, *what an intelligent man, I wasn't able to make out a single word of what he said,* and all the while the con artist runs off to another conference hall to repeat the same gobbledegook and receive the same ovation. I'll never go again.

To make matters worse, I used to sit in the last row,

at the end of the hall that was always very long and very narrow, and the voice of the lecturer would reach me like a rivulet of urine running under the feet of the public. After a while I'd be bored and would cast my eyes around (my eyes that are cerulean in the centre and violet around the edges), and pray to God that the conference would come to an end, and when it finally came to an end I'd stand up and leave in a hurry as if I were terribly late for an appointment. But once in the street I'd walk home slowly, all on my own, peering into shop-windows to delay the moment of coming home and having to prepare a meal for myself alone. And let me tell you something else, Gianfranco, let me warn you: conferences are attended by a certain kind of men whose only purpose is to approach solitary women. They sit next to them, rub an elbow or a knee against them, start a conversation, offer them a mint and then pretend to invite them to have a coffee together. But it's just another trap. They charm them, suggest a rendezvous and then never reappear, never phone them again, leave them to die of anguish and shame at a downtown street corner.

Nor will I attend any more art exhibits. The openings are taken over by sinister people standing with their backs to the wall and to the paintings, talking and talking and smoking and not even glancing at the paintings; they hide the paintings with their bodies and their smoke, and when the opening is over at last, they all leave at once and the paintings appear scratched, cracked, smudged, chipped, ruined. I can't understand how painters allow the public at these exhibits to sabotage their work in this way. And after the opening, no one goes to the gallery, because who wants to see those atrocities, all old and discoloured? A solitary pensioner with nowhere to go, spinsters, old men who come in to seek refuge from the rain or the cold and who totter past the paintings as they would past a row of prisoners amongst whom they must identify the murderer of their daughter. They glance at them sideways, hurriedly, with distrust and fear, and finally they escape into the street rather than become the victims of these ghastly works of art.

I, in a single day, have been to five or six of these exhibits of 'posthumous' paintings. I've observed each canvas to the point of hatred, to the point of no longer seeing it, I've observed from near and from far, I've observed sitting down and standing up, I've scrutinized a canvas as if I suspected it of being a fake or as if I were trying to discover, under the coarse brushstrokes, a lost Renaissance madonna. And all because when I've finished looking at them and standing up and sitting down and consulting the catalogue, I have to walk back all alone, and I stop in front of the shop-windows so as not to have to go home and prepare a sad apple-compote.

Sometimes, in a corner of the gallery, I'd see the artist, the author of those paintings, almost always accompanied by an ugly, disagreeable, very masculine woman. The artist would watch me, would spy on me to see my reaction. My God, the impudence of these artists who want to discover us with our mouths open in admiration or with our eyes enthralled as we admire their paintings! Every time I'd see one of them there, preying like a ruffian on my comings and goings in front of his work, I'd become furious and on purpose I'd pull a consternated face and avoid looking back at him, until suddenly, after the third or fourth painting, I'd turn violently around and fix my eyes on him, and leave the exhibition fuming as if I'd gone into the men's room by mistake.

On the street I never stop at the shop-windows with female mannequins. I detest these tall, blonde young women with golden eyelids. I could stare at them for days with a serpent's eye, and they'd still be smiling scornfully, mocking me because they dress in the latest fashion and I walk about in my five-year-old clothes. Nor do I stop in front of the male mannequins. I'm afraid of those young men with their long, blond hair, light-brown faces, pupils lit up by a drug-induced brilliance and the bodies so hard and so trim. There are: tall, frightening, ready to jump on me. I walk past them with my head lowered, trying not to be seen.

Instead, I'm attracted to the windows of grocery stores: all those bottles, all those jars, those boxes of candied fruit, of black prunes and raisins, the tins of sweets. *Ultramarine*. What a beautiful word, Gianfranco. Ultramarine shops.

But the windows I prefer are those that nobody looks at, badly lit, as sad as a room whose occupant has died and that no one has touched since, windows with orthopaedic contraptions, syringes or pumice stones. I see them so lonely and despised that I always stop to look at them, and imagine that these are places created on purpose for us solitary beings to meet. Sometimes a man will stop and stare too, at my same window. And you know what, Gianfranco? Between that man and I there establishes itself a subtle link, a sympathy, a communion. We don't need to speak. We both enjoy feeling that we are set aside from the crowds that stare at the mannequin windows. The truth is that we're not interested in the orthopaedic contraptions nor in the abrasives nor in the insecticides, but we look at them with deep-felt sorrow because no one except us looks at them. That is our mission: to take upon ourselves that which the others despise.

I need to leave, Gianfranco. Leave and go to a city where we poets are like prostitutes: where we can walk down the street and men will follow us and, in a low voice, offer us money, not to make love to them but to recite poetry. How much does a ticket to Paris cost? A hundred thousand pesos? How will I find that kind of money? Who will lend it to me or give it to me as a gift? Where will I steal it from? I'll sell my jewels, my Leipzig piano, my English china and go somewhere far, far away. Or I'll become a stowaway. Buenos Aires is not a poet's city. Here every man fixes his eyes on a point to my right or to my left, never on me. I advance among those looks as through a tunnel opened for myself alone. How funny, I'm the invisible woman! Gianfranco: I hope God is somewhere between myself and the end of the tunnel, otherwise I think I'll go crazy.

At last I know who you remind me of. You remind me of Le Clézio, that French novelist so young and so handsome, whose photograph I saw in the literary supplement of *La Nación*. But Le Clézio has eyes that are blue around the edges and grey in the centre: cold, ironic eyes—even cruel, I believe. Yours are ardent and passionate, and at the same time as chaste as those of a child. When we met at the bookstore L'Amateur, you approached me and asked me to sign a copy of *The Faces of Death* that you had just bought from the salesman who had no doubt told you that there was the author and pointed at me with his finger. You added in a low voice, as if you were confiding a secret, *my name is Gianfranco,* and then I looked you in the eyes and wrote: 'To Gianfranco whose eyes are green in the centre and golden around the edges,' and you liked that very much. Then we left the bookstore together and walked until all the streets suddenly changed names.

I was wearing, I still remember, my fur coat, and you were wearing grey flannel trousers, a white turtle-neck, a honey-coloured sports jacket, oxblood moccasins and blue socks with a red stripe. In the street, the women glared at us; they seemed to be hurling at you wordless and terrible accusations. But you paid no attention to them. You walked on as if making way for me, as if removing obstacles from my path. The others would step aside and you and I would walk as if along a carpet unrolled exclusively for the two of us. I reached your chin and yet I'm a tall woman, hair the colour of blood and a deep voice like Lauren Bacall's. When the streets changed names we realized we were dead tired and we entered a café, and you continued to make way for me until we reached a little table set in a corner among wooden flower-boxes and artificial plants.

A *belle époque* café, you said. You asked the waiter for two coffees but the waiter made a mistake or didn't make a mistake and brought us two cognacs just as if we'd been at the bistro round the corner from Madame Pomargue's hotel. We laughed and then slowly sipped our drinks, watching one another in order to adjust our movements. Then an orchestra, up in one of the balconies, started playing Brahms. You took the book and read in a low voice all my poems. Then you closed it with the gestures of a priest manipulating a sacred object, laid it down, put your elbows on the table, leaned your chin on your hands and looked at me. And at that very moment we realized we loved one another because we both loved poetry. But you didn't ask me to kiss you, like the men at the conferences, nor did you leave me on my own like those who stare with me at the orthopaedic legs and the bits of metal. You stayed by my side until all the lights were extinguished.

And if I flew to New York? Even if I know that in New York I'd melt like a lump of sugar in hot water. Better Paris. Paris or Rome or London. No, not London, never London. *Ô quelle ville de la Bible.* In London I'd die strangled by a Jack the Ripper with a light-brown face and long hair. Don't worry, I'll travel. I must never again be a woman who, in the waiting-room of a train station, pretends to wait for the arrival or departure of a train, while she sits there like a beggar or a prostitute.

The men who loved me eight or ten years ago no longer exist for me. Even if they wished to marry me I'd tell them that I don't think badly of them but that I simply don't love them. Juan Carlos Birelli disappeared for the last time after asking me in the Jockey Club Tea Room to go with him to a hotel where rooms are rented by the hour, and I wouldn't go, and I never saw him again, and he never wrote or phoned since that afternoon when I drank a grapefruit juice and he a coffee. I can't love him. I don't even know if I like him or if I let myself be kissed two or three times just to interrupt my loneliness.

It's terrible, Gianfranco. It's terrible to pretend not to see the defects of the man who is holding your hand. Until one day you can't take it any longer and then you feel like throwing up.

Have I ever told you about Julio Wialicki? He was very young, very tall, very blond, very pale but with the red lips of a woman. We met six times in the café at Paraguay and Maipú. Three of the times I've forgotten; the other three, I wish I could forget. He had ashen eyes in the centre and also around the edges, and when I caressed him a sort of whirlpool would appear in the ashes. When he saw me come in, he'd rise to his feet, kiss my cheek with his damp rubber lips, he'd help me take off my coat and tell me how elegant I looked, and how well the Titian-coloured hair suited me. But he never looked at me; he would always be looking towards the other tables as if he sought or feared someone else's presence, and after a while he'd become cross and I could tell then that he hated me. Until I discovered that his searching looks would be directed more than once at certain young boys in jeans. For that reason I said goodbye to him forever without telling him why I was saying goodbye, nor did he ask me, and for many years now I wake thinking about him or I fall asleep thinking about him, but I don't despise him—even if I don't love him.

You don't kiss me on the cheek or on the mouth, you don't ask me to go with you to a hotel, you've never said *how elegant you look,* and when I grew a fringe and cut it off unevenly you said nothing either. But you hold my right hand in your right hand, carry it to your left arm, allow it to rest there and press it hard with your arm against your body, and then I can feel the heat of your body, your young feline muscles. But what about the exhibitions I attend all alone? And the conferences I listen to alone without understanding them and without even wanting to hear them? And the shop-windows where the mannequins display dresses that I will never be able to afford? And my friends, where are my friends, silent as sleeping waves? Why don't they publish my poems any more in the literary supplements? Why, every time I take them a poem, do they make me wait for hours in those cold tiled waiting-rooms, and instead of seeing me send clerks to walk by me and keep an unobtrusive eye on me? I no longer publish. Now I write only for myself and for those who will read me a hundred years from now. Of *The Faces of Death,* ninety-three copies were sold, and one of those I found in a second-hand bookstore on Avenida

Corrientes, still carrying my inscription. The name of the person to whom I had inscribed it had been effaced, but I know who it was. It was either Julio Wialicki or Juan Carlos Birelli. I bought the book and brought it home with me, and there where the name had been effaced I wrote in yours, Gianfranco.

Now publishers want me to put up I don't know how many thousands of pesos to publish *The Games of Madness*. They say that books of poetry don't sell. They're right. But poetry is for me as speech is for others; I can't remain silent forever. I see the objects of my love or fear go by, and I need to yell out to them, I need to call them to me or shoo them away, and the publishers come and tell me I'm wrong, that I should remain silent because they don't earn money with my voices, with my voice, with the only voice I have to speak to others and to myself. They condemn me to a soliloquy, Gianfranco. But a continuous soliloquy is like a continuous dialogue: in both directions lies madness. No matter. I know that a hundred years hence my poetry will be the language of humankind. This isn't vanity, Gianfranco. Without the illusion of glory no one would write anything. And sometimes, as you see, we are satisfied with the illusion of that illusion, with posthumous glory. How heroic or how stupid we poets are! True enough. My writing changes colour here because I'm changing pens. The previous ballpoint ran out.

I've heard that when someone wears mourning it seems to that someone that there are more people wearing mourning than ever before. With me it's the other way round. When Daddy was alive and I had no money problems, I used to see poor people all over the place. Now the poor have vanished, the women who used to walk the streets with tiny babies in their arms and had nothing to eat and nowhere to sleep have become respectable housewives. And I'm the only one who walks the streets, round and round again. For me there are no jobs, no invitations, no husbands, no fiancés, no friends, no cars, no jewels, no letters, no phone calls. I ask myself how all those people manage to make for themselves a little corner in this world, a nest, and I instead am like a stray, lost sheep. Sometimes I believe that God forged this destiny for me. God hasn't wanted anything to distract me from poetry. And that leads me to believe that, if that is so, then my poetry is as good as Baudelaire's or Pavese's. But at what cost, Gianfranco! To write *The Faces of Death,* to write *The Games of Madness,* and then to go crazy and die.

When I received the poetry prize I had my fifteen minutes of invitations, friendships, even rendezvous arranged over the phone. Everyone wanted to know me. I thought they were coming to me just as I was going to them, to live out what we were writing. Gianfranco,

I know that I don't distinguish myself from those who are not poets merely because of what I write. I know that the difference spreads to my face, to my gestures, even to my clothes, and to my tastes, and to my ideas, to my whole self. That is why in no time at all I had plunged myself into silence, and the women, with the expression of having heard next door the cries of a sick person and wishing to pretend that nothing had happened, would talk all at the same time of their trips to Europe, of the scandal of an ill-conceived literary prize or of the senile love affairs of a celebrated writer. The men stared at them as if they, the women, were repeating a lesson that they, the men, had taught them; every so often they, the men, would correct a name, a date, but they'd also exchange glances among themselves to agree about something or to remind each other of something, and then one of the two men, or both of the men who had exchanged glances would look in my direction, discreetly, as if to check that I was still there and that they hadn't made a mistake. And I, silent, smiling without wanting to smile, stopped understanding the conversation of those women who kept interrupting one another as if to prevent the cries of the sick person next door from being heard. And then they'd all say goodbye with the promise of phoning one another and of seeing one another in some other place, and in the street they'd shake my hand and congratulate me on my poems and my prize, and then they'd climb into their cars and I'd find myself walking home all on my own once again.

I often meet them at the conferences and in the waiting-rooms of the periodicals. We pretend not to recognize one another. When the conference is over and I get up and leave, I hear them behind my back inviting each other to dinners at embassies and cocktails at the Cinzano Club, but I continue to go out on my own, continue to walk on my own down the street and stop at a shop-window of orthopaedic contraptions, and sometimes buy myself a chocolate bar and eat it slowly with tears in my eyes. In the waiting-rooms of the periodicals I stare fixedly at a wall while they, the women, shower me with their Christian Dior perfumes and they, the men, with their scent of blond tobacco, citrus fruit and precious woods. The clerks greet them and watch me with hostility. Someone opens a door, calls them by their first names or nicknames, they hug, they kiss, they shake hands, they laugh and finally they disappear into the deep recesses of the carpeted offices, and I stand up and leave with my latest poem in my handbag.

Nor do I wish to join those old men and women who meet in some funereal café on Avenida de Mayo. I hate them. Once they dragged me along, they asked me if I liked the verses of Bartrina or Lorenzo Stechetti, they recited for me their hosts of daffodils. On another occasion, they asked me to read my poems, and I, fed up, recited for them Duhamel's 'Ballad of Florentin Prunier,' and they looked at me with consternation or smiled indulgently, and one old man, undulating like a thick soup, assured me that I reminded him of that ancient Argentine classic, Guido Spano. Then I stood up and left and never returned. But I'm afraid they'll come after me. I'm afraid they'll grab hold of my unpublished poems and turn them into acrostics or into ballads *à la* García Lorca. I hate them even more than I hate the others. Because the others simply reject me, and at least rejected I keep myself intact, but these old people take me in only to smother me in their jellies.

Gianfranco, am I condemned to write all on my own, to read all on my own, to live all on my own, to be the sister of Aloysius Bertrand and the Count of Lautréamont, and all those great spirits, the sister who understands every single one of their secret words, who shares each of their tremors? Am I condemned to become a strange and solitary woman who can't expect—I don't say love—but even sympathy or concern from anyone? Does being a great artist in the eyes of posterity require being something repulsive in the eyes of one's contemporaries? And please don't list the cases to the contrary. Leave me with the idea that my face, my gestures, my ridiculous behaviour win me points in the court of the god of poetry. Or does that god not allow himself to be bribed? Is he indifferent to our suffering, Gianfranco? As indifferent as the universe? Is it we who believe that suffering guarantees compensation? And are we wrong?

Enoch Soames. Have you read that terrifying story by Max Beerbohm? Am I to be another Enoch Soames, an Enoch Soames who sold her life to suffering in the hope of being the subject of studies, essays, anthologies, a hundred years hence, and a hundred years hence I won't even have the consolation of seeing myself transformed into the heroine of a short story? But I have you, Gianfranco. And you, you who love Aloysius Bertrand and the Count of Lautréamont, and wept when I recited for you the 'Ballad of Florentin Prunier,' you also love my poems and are not alarmed by my hallucinated eyes, by my dress and my gorgon hair. Thank you, Gianfranco. You, who are my contemporary, are also my posterity. You are that secret young man who would allow himself to be killed for the sake of my books.

I'm writing this letter to you in an exercise book. It's three o'clock in the afternoon. A week ago I travelled to Mar del Plata. Did you know that in these past few years I've travelled to that seaside resort every three months, but never in the summer? I travel alone by bus, I stay alone in a miserable hotel on La Perla beach, I walk alone down the promenade, alone I look at the sea, alone I eat in a restaurant on Calle Belgrano (where they don't lay out tablecloths but use paper coverings, and I often have to share my table with elderly couples or single men who look up at me only once and then never again). In the afternoon I walk alone along the desolate downtown streets, I buy myself a small sweet pastry, and at four or five I go to the casino. I play roulette. I win, I lose, I win and lose again. I leave the casino alone, I buy myself another pastry, I walk back alone to the hotel on La Perla, I go to bed alone, alone I listen to the bellowing of the sea and alone I fall asleep.

But last week I went to Mar del Plata with a hundred thousand pesos. The bank clerk told me not to close the account, to leave at least a thousand to my credit, but I paid no attention to him and withdrew all the money I had. I was fed up with going every month and withdrawing a small sum and then walking by all those shop-windows. I could see in my bank-book the balance of my account quickly diminishing. First, when Daddy died, it seemed like an enormous sum that would last me for as long as I lived. Then every month there was less, less, less. That was when I started reading the classified ads. Until last week I'd had enough (as I just said) and went to the bank and took out all my savings. It was almost a hundred thousand pesos. I thought I'd win at the casino and with my winnings I'd pay for the printing of *The Games of Madness,* and I'd still have enough to keep me for another few years, until they decided to give me the National Literary Prize and my pension. And perhaps *The Games of Madness* would become a bestseller, would sell more copies than *Gone With The Wind* and *Love Story,* and I'd earn fabulous amounts of money. Don't laugh, Gianfranco. All we authors think the same.

I took the bus that leaves Constitución at 2:25 p.m. Fortunately, no one sat next to me. Throughout the whole trip I looked out of the window. At one of the stops I ate a chocolate bar and at another I drank a grapefruit juice. We arrived in Mar del Plata after dark; at nine o'clock that night I was already at the casino. I didn't go to the hotel on La Perla. I had no suitcase, no luggage at all, only my handbag with 96,300 pesos. By eleven o'clock I'd lost everything except the money for the return fare. At 11:15 I was at the terminal. The bus was scheduled to leave at 12:55. I waited there alone, as if instead of being the woman I am I was a woman without a soul and without a name. I don't know how I managed to remain so silent, so very alone and so very hungry. Since eating that chocolate bar at four and drinking that grapefruit juice at seven, no food or drink passed my lips until I got home next morning. I must be a whore (excuse my language, Gianfranco) or a human angel, because in the half-dark windswept terminal I felt almost contented thinking that I'm good, that everything would change some day or night, and that my intimate world was still untouched by those whom I don't want groping at it. I didn't catch a glimpse of the sea, neither from near nor from afar, but I heard it cry out like a wounded whale. I travelled back to Buenos Aires sleeping softly. Without happiness, but without asking anything from anyone. I felt I was in a glass bell travelling alone through space.

I've fallen asleep again and now I've woken up and I don't know what the time is. I forgot to wind up my watch and the watch shows a time I don't understand, the hands open at an absurd angle. I rang up the operator to ask for the time, and I couldn't make out what the stupid woman was mumbling between her teeth. The radio stations are either silent or are broadcasting identical music. I can hear no sounds on the street or in the rest of the house. Maybe everyone is asleep because it's nighttime, maybe it's daytime and everyone is dead or gone. The shutters of my room are closed. I write by the light of the night-lamp. But you haven't left your room, isn't that right? You carry on reading my letter and as soon as I finish writing it and you finish reading it, you'll give me a call, you'll say *My dear, I'm on my way,* and you'll arrive laden with parcels and flowers.

The silence is as deep as a well into which everything falls from very high above. I don't want to leave my bed and open the shutters and look outside. I prefer to imagine myself alone in the city. Everyone has departed a long time ago, leaving me on my own, playing with my poems as if they were coins no longer in circulation. Once upon a time they gave me the poetry prize to satisfy me and to keep me in my place. Then they all went off to enjoy themselves on all the côtes d'azur in the world, and I, like a sick little girl, stayed home writing my poetry, all alone. I know that when I'm dead they'll return and grab hold of my poems as if they were a newly discovered treasure. But in the meantime I'm alive, Gianfranco, I'm alive and I'm alone! And from my loneliness I hear the commotion of the world like that of a party to which I haven't been invited. My God, this seems like a poor imitation of a lachrymose and didactic poem! Forgive me, Gianfranco. Let's change the subject. When you arrive, ring three times, that way I'll know it's you. Bring me a box of candied fruit. I have a yearning for candied fruit. And chocolates. And a bottle of white wine. I'm thirsty.

Maybe while I was sleeping the phone rang and I didn't hear it, and it was Julio Wialicki. I met Julio Wialicki (or was it Juan Carlos Birelli? I no longer remember or care to remember) in a bookstore. A salesman told him that I was the author of *The Faces of Death*; they had just given me the prize, and he bought it and brought it over to me for an inscription. But he never read my poems out loud to me, and the fourth or fifth time we met I began to realize that he didn't understand, and felt as if I were sitting next to an incurable invalid, letting him think he was in full health. I love neither of them, and if they asked me to marry them, I'd say no.

As my hand started aching from so much writing, I stopped for a while. The ceiling continues to shower me with its angry or distracted spittle. That is the inconvenience of living on the top floor of an apartment building. On the radio, insomniac broadcasters have started to babble and are saying that it's two o'clock, three o'clock in the morning. As soon as I got back from Mar del Plata I rummaged through all the drawers, through all the pockets of my dresses, through all the handbags and purses and vases and sewing-baskets, but I couldn't find a single centavo; all I found was the savings-account booklet with the official stamp on the cover, and on every page the red seal that cried out *cancelled, cancelled, cancelled.* The last three hundred pesos I spent on a taxi from Constitución and even gave the driver twenty pesos as a tip, because he was a young man, blond, although I couldn't see his eyes because he didn't turn round once to look at me. I asked him if he liked poetry and he said yes. I asked him if he had read *The Faces of Death* and he answered that all he had ever read were the tango lyrics of Homero Manzi. I wasn't offended as I was with the fossils in that mortuary café on Avenida de Mayo. Manzi was a real poet, and how nice that even taxi drivers read him. I asked him what his name was and he said Gianfranco.

Now I'm very tired but not sleepy. I sense that dawn is breaking. I know that it's dawn because all things have begun to slim down and stretch like hungry cats. From the street comes the sound of cars fleeing in all directions. You are still sitting by the fire, reading me. But you're no longer blond. Neither blond nor young. Suddenly I've discovered that all blond young men turn their eyes away when they see me. You have dark hair and you're about fifty. Your name I won't change because I like those Italian names that end in *o* and have an *r* in the middle. Nor did I meet you in a bookstore, what nonsense! I met you next to table thirty-eight at the casino. My chips were cerulean like the centre of my eyes and yours were green like the centre of yours. There where I placed a cerulean chip you placed a green one, and that is how we watched one another without watching one another for a very long time. We would both win, we would both lose, we would both win and lose again, and all the time, on the felt, your green eye would watch my cerulean eye. Until your golden eye looked at my violet eye and we smiled. Since that moment, you're Gianfranco.

I know you won't come visit me until I finish writing this letter. But I don't want to finish writing it because when I finish it I'll have to start thinking about what I'll do tomorrow to go on living. I'll stand in the atrium of the church of San Nicolás de Bari, and when a matron walks by, one of those matrons who enter as if hiding under their mantillas, cluttered with rosaries and missals, I'll confront her with my eyes of deep hunger and madness on the surface, and the matron, frightened, will give me money without my asking for it. Or I'll stand all day long at a corner of Avenida Corrientes until, at nightfall, a man dressed in a charioteer's black overcoat, smelling foully of psoriasis and of ancient mothballs, will stop by my side, will make a pained face as if wishing to relieve himself, will pretend to watch the cars pass and finally will turn and hang on to me with the rusty hooks of his eyes. Then I'll smile at him, I'll start walking away and the man will come following at my heels. Or I'll phone Juan Carlos Birelli, I'll tell him I agree to accompany him to the hotel, and once in the room I'll murder him and steal his wallet. I have nothing to pawn. The piano isn't from Leipzig, it's worth nothing, it's moth-ridden and several of its strings are missing. My jewels are cheap paste. And my china isn't china, just vulgar crockery. I won't let go of my books even if I starve. And even sitting in a train station I'll continue to write my poems on old newspaper pages. Don't you understand, Gianfranco? I'll resign myself to all sorts of martyrdoms just to be able to bet on the possibility, faint at best, that people whom I'll never know inherit what I now collect with blood and tears.

But also, why deny it, I think of that Le Clézio so blond, so young and so handsome. And then I tell myself that my oddness is not, as I often boast to console myself, a guarantee of anything. That to believe that I've exchanged today's executioners for tomorrow's devotees is the saddest of my fantasies, perhaps a sterile and resentful boast. And yet, if even now the Devil were to appear and suggest transforming me, in exchange for my soul, into a young and beautiful woman, the first thing I'd ask him is if I'd still be the secret sister of Aloysius Bertrand and of Pavese, and if the Devil were to say no, I'd turn him down. You see, I'm like those homosexuals who suffer the kicks of society, and if they were to be born again they'd still choose to be homosexuals.

I no longer know what to write to you, Gianfranco. My fingers are all stiff. I won't go to Europe. I'll go to a small country in Central America where the people are very sweet, very poor, very kind-hearted. I'll wear linen dresses and sandals, and will plait my hair into one long braid down to my feet. I'll take on the name of a dark woman, fleshy and sensual. I'll call myself Aglonga Gonuyaz. I'll be Memé Albaquime. In the mornings I'll teach the children to read and write, and the parents will pay me with baskets of fruit and preserves. I'll take walks every afternoon along beaches tattooed by the waves, at the edge of a sapphire sea. And at night, lying in a hammock beneath the chaste giraffe-necked palm trees, I'll compose pantheistic hymns. Handsome and adolescent mulattos, with skin the colour of rich veins, will follow me everywhere like mesmerized tigers. They'll watch over my sleep like insomniac guard-dogs. My beauty will be a sun that will bronze them deeper than the sun in the sky. During the day their eyes will seem like charred pebbles. At night they'll shine like feverish fireflies. But during the day I'll walk among them without looking at them, tall, haughty, immaculate, like a Virgin carried in procession on a platform. And at night, wrapped up in a mosquito-net as if in a cloud of incense, I'll fall asleep more chaste than the palm trees.

The ink of the ballpoint pen is beginning to pale. Before it runs out completely I want to tell you, Gianfranco, that this letter isn't a letter. Nor do you exist, nor does this woman, so crazy and so unhappy. In fifteen or twenty days, in some magazine, in some literary supplement, a story will be published, a story called 'Letter to Gianfranco.' It will include this same paragraph that I now include to disconcert the readers.

Or perhaps the woman did exist, but they found her dead in her room, dead of hunger, literally, or poisoned with sleeping-pills. In her hands—no, that's too purple—on the night-table was the exercise book in which she had written this laborious monologue. Someone, let's say one of her friends, one of those men who called her once on the phone and then never again, arrived summoned by the police—she had his phone number written down somewhere—picked up the exercise book, immediately saw the opportunity of using it as a story, changed names and places, altered a few sentences and finally published this 'Letter to Gianfranco' as his own invention.

Or let's admit that he wasn't a crook. Let's imagine that instead he felt the pinprick of guilt, was invaded by remorse, wanted to slap himself and slap all those who like himself had not known how to be the imaginary Gianfranco, and published the letter—corrected of course, so that the author would not be recognized, a useless precaution because, as the song has it, many are the poets who could put their name to these words.

There's another possibility, Gianfranco. That this letter is indeed a letter and that you are indeed its recipient. You've received it, you've read it, and after rewriting it, after eliminating the compromising details, after substituting my adjectives for yours and changing your name for that of Gianfranco, whom you insist on presenting as a fictional character, you shamelessly publish it, without knowing that you've fallen into the trap I've sprung for you: you'll be my Max Beerbohm.

And who then has written this last page that apparently reveals either a theft or a literary device, and in which certain changes of meaning are so evident? I, the woman of flesh and blood, or you? I, to have my anticipated revenge on you—and you don't destroy the page because, being a writer, you cannot resist the temptation of making the readers believe that fictional characters exist? Or you, for that very same reason, because you enjoy that ambiguity that, pointing at the same time to both reality and the imagination, lies at the root of all literature?

Enough, Gianfranco. However fascinating you find these games (these sleights of hand, your detractors will say), they interest no one but yourself. A woman of blood and suffering, or a phantom of words and smoke: it makes no difference. The only thing your readers demand is that you don't deceive them with tears of wax. And both you and I know that my tears contain all the bitterness of the sea.

And now farewell, Gianfranco. You can now leave that room where I held you prisoner for one day and one night. It's morning, the sun is shining, the weather's fine. I hope that I'll have enough ink in the pen to sign, at the bottom of this last page, my name.

In days gone by, the building had been occupied by affluent families. Then, one after the other, the apartments had been let to stockbrokers, customs brokers, trust companies. But Henriette and Leopoldina von Wels had preferred not to move. At night, they and Hildstrut, their old Hungarian servant, were the only living souls in the building, because even Wilson, the caretaker, slept away in his house in Montserrat. They weren't afraid to be left on their own and, to tell the truth, they quite enjoyed it.

During the day there was a discreet coming and going of people, and the place was rather boisterous. But from nine in the evening onwards, the building was steeped in the silence and darkness of an abandoned mine. Only on the eighth floor was there light and, quite often, a soft music. If one of the tenants had been in his office at those hours, he'd have said: 'That's the two foreigners up there.'

Henriette would read, Leopoldina would embroider or crochet a mat. On the monumental gramophone a record would turn: Mozart, Schubert, Schumann,

Chopin, Liszt and, from time to time, Wagner (but Leopoldina, even though she never said so, detested Wagner and didn't dare confess her preference for Rossini). If the weather was warm, they'd go out on the balcony. In summer, all their friends would leave for the beaches, and if they themselves went nowhere during the warm months it was because the slightest effort affected Leopoldina's health.

This was what they did on that particular night: go out on the balcony and enjoy the view. Once, Leopoldina had made a very accurate observation:

'Have you noticed, Henriette? No one lives across the road. They're nothing but transients on the other side of the Avenida Leandro Alem.'

True enough. What lay in front of their eyes was a city with no stable population: the train station of Retiro, the Plaza Britanica, the Sheraton Hotel, the towers of Las Catalinas Norte, the docks and, far back, the river. But at night, winter and summer, the spectacle was fascinating, almost unreal.

Buenos Aires seemed empty, languid, as if it had not yet recovered from the commotions of New Year's Eve. Along Leandro Alem slid a few lost cars. Only the towers of Las Catalinas, resplendent at night with their black polish, had kept a few stories lit up like silver Christmas wreaths. In the background, the lights of the dockyards blinked in a cloudy gloom. And above, a vast open sky such as one rarely sees in a large city. Henriette and Leopoldina, leaning on the balustrade, were thinking of nothing in particular.

Then they heard the music. It came from behind them, as if from within their own apartment. But they hadn't put a record on the gramophone. And it wasn't classical music either: it was a tango. A tango played on an accordion. They looked at each other in astonishment. Henriette decided that it had to be a radio. But who had turned a radio on at this hour and in their building? And no, it wasn't a radio: an error in the execution was corrected, a phrase was repeated three times, as if to learn it by heart.

Henriette went back into the apartment and walked out into the entrance hall. Where was she headed? What was she going to do? Leopoldina followed her. On each floor there was a covered gallery that led from the entrance hall to the kitchen and to the servants' quarters. Protected by a wall of frosted glass, it opened onto a deep air-vent that occupied the full height of the building, and through which sounds from the lower apartments rose during the day, and silence and darkness drifted up at night. Henriette climbed onto a chair and leaned over the glass wall. Deep down in the vent, at the level of the seventh floor, she could see a mist of yellow light.

They returned to the living-room and sat down.

They looked at each other as if formulating a question. The sound of the accordion seemed to float in mid-air, emanating from the walls, from the floor, from the ceiling, like that music called functional usually found in certain up-to-date offices and in the waiting-rooms of some surgeries, springing from who-knows-where.

'Who could it be?' whispered Leopoldina.

Henriette answered impatiently:

'To begin with, it's a man. Women don't play the accordion.'

But she hadn't lifted her voice, she too had whispered. She stood up, and walking on tiptoe she switched off all the lights, leaving lit only a small mushroom of coloured glass. Then she returned to her seat.

That first night, the concert lasted a good half-hour. The two Misses Wels knew nothing about tango, believing it to be a vulgar and somewhat objectionable genre. But music is music and night is night, and the combination of the two always gives birth to a delicate mystery. They listened without saying a word, without moving, breathing softly and rhythmically as if they were sleeping. Slowly they discovered two things: that the accordion is not a musical instrument, it's almost a human voice, and that with no elements other than its music, the tango tells a story. That first night the stories were love stories, not tragic or passionate love stories but rather playful, and even tender, like the stories of a youthful love affair.

After that, nothing. Nothing for a long while. Then they were startled by a slamming door, followed by the sudden jolt of the elevator when it's summoned from one of the upper stories and is still on the ground floor. At night everything can be heard. They heard the elevator stop, the grill door open and close, then the elevator start off once again. And at last they heard a second slamming door, this one further away, on the street.

Henriette ran to the balcony and looked over, Leopoldina at her heels. But the building had been erected over the arched passageway of Leandro Alem, and the balcony was a metre wider than the passageway. Even if one leaned out with half the body, one would still not have been able to make out the edge of the curb. If someone left the building and walked away under the arches, it was utterly impossible to see him from above. No car, no taxi stopped by the curb, and no one crossed the avenue on foot, so it became apparent that whoever had left the building had used the arched passageway. Was it the same person who minutes before had been playing the accordion?

Henriette went back to have a look: the vent was in pitch darkness. Yes, it must have been the same person. The two Misses Wels waited on the balcony without breathing a word. Midnight came, and as Henriette didn't seem inclined to go to bed, Leopoldina was able to continue to tinker with the idea that had suddenly struck her: the man had been playing the accordion for them, the music was a cyphered message, the message said *'I've arrived, I'm here,'* and after sending it, he had left. Would he be back?

Next morning, Hildstrut, instead of finding out from Wilson, as they had instructed her to do, who was renting the seventh-floor apartment, allowed that vulgar and gossiping man who liked to arch his body and lift his buttocks in an obscene manner, to come and inform them in person.

He told them that the new tenant was a young man. He had moved into the seventh-floor apartment on the previous afternoon, a quick and simple move: only a few sticks of furniture, but lots and lots of baskets, and hangers with clothes of bright colours, as well as several tuxedos. Apparently he lived on his own.

'I don't know what he wants with such a big apartment. You wait and see: that boy will cause trouble.'

'What sort of trouble?' asked Henriette in a haughty tone. Wilson didn't appear to be in the least intimidated.

'You can well imagine. I've got a good eye when it comes to people. That boy is a nightbird. Handsome, pale skin, greased-down hair and outfits that are not meant for office-work.'

Henriette felt annoyed.

72

'Obviously the apartments are rented out to any kind of riff-raff.'

Wilson was staring at them, staring at them and not leaving, keen to see what impression his words had made. Leopoldina tried hard not to betray the slightest gesture.

'I bet,' Wilson said, 'that at night he invites his buddies and lots of women, and they live it up in style. And who's going to complain? You two are the only ones here.'

'If there's any commotion we'll let the office know,' Henriette answered, more icily than a Habsburg dismissing a servant. 'You may go now, Wilson.'

When at last they got rid of the nuisance, Hildstrut, who because she was somewhat deaf had not heard the music, said:

'It's much better if there are other people in the building at night.'

This incensed Henriette.

'That depends on the kind of people.'

Leopoldina made no comment. But Henriette noticed in her a tremor of excitement. Was it possible that Leopoldina was frightened? That same afternoon, Henriette called the locksmith and had him install a second latch on the front door.

♦

No trouble of any kind. During the day it was impossible to make out, in the midst of so much noise, the sounds that might have been coming from the seventh floor. At night the lights were on, but no sounds could be heard then either, no conversations. And around ten, the accordion. Tangos, always tangos. Around eleven, he would leave. Where to? To play at some nightclub? Probably.

'I'm sure he's an accordionist in a group somewhere,' Henriette would say. 'What I don't understand is why he's come to live here. Normally these people live in the suburbs.'

Leopoldina continued to not make any comment.

And Sundays he obviously spent sleeping or in someone else's house, because on Sundays there were no lights turned on and no accordion concerts, and the ladies would quarrel over the most trivial things.

The other nights, a few minutes before ten, they'd both be sitting alert in the living-room armchairs. Henriette pretended to read, but for some reason wouldn't put a record on the gramophone. Leopoldina embroidered or did her crochet, but every so often she'd drop a stitch.

As soon as the first syllables could be heard—because these were syllables, mouthed by the accordion— Henriette would mutter in a tone that aspired to be ironic or dismissive:

'Well, he's at it again with his serenade. *Eine kleine Nachtmusik* of the suburbs.'

But she'd forget to turn the pages of her book and, after a while, she'd close her eyes and put the book down on her knees. Leopoldina would interrupt her labours, would rest her neck on the top edge of the armchair, and through the window would gaze upon the starry sky.

As the nights went by, Leopoldina reached the conclusion that the music was a cry for help. The boy was saying to them *'I'm lonesome, I'm sad,'* and then he'd be silent because he'd be waiting for an answer, and then, because the answer wouldn't come, he'd go out, not to a nightclub but to wander alone through the streets. He'd probably return at dawn or at sunrise, when the building had woken, and that is why she, Leopoldina, even if she stayed up all night, never heard him come home.

One night she was unable to stand it any longer and said:

'There are certain tangos that I like.'

Henriette's reaction was so extreme that Leopoldina guessed the truth.

'How can you like that music?' wheezed Henriette, apparently suffering from a sudden asthma attack. 'Please! That music belongs in the slums!'

Leopoldina guessed that Henriette was furious because she too liked the tangos.

One day, before going back home, Wilson appeared

bearing a big smile.

'So? How's the heartbreaker on the seventh floor behaving these days?'

Henriette pretended to be amused:

'Why do you call him a heartbreaker?'

Wilson, without breaking his smile, screwed up his porcine eyes like a short-sighted person trying to improve his sight.

'You've never seen him?'

'No, of course, never.'

'Doesn't he ever bother you, at night?'

'Not at all. If it weren't for what you told us, we'd say that the seventh floor was still empty.'

'Well, what do you know! And I imagined him to be a playboy!'

'A what?'

'No, nothing. It's that he's so good-looking. Just like a movie star.'

Would they never see him, not even from a distance, from the balcony?

One night, in the darkness of the bedroom, so that Henriette wouldn't dissuade her with the merest glance, Leopoldina found the courage to say it.

'We should meet him.'

'Meet him? And how?' Henriette hadn't asked 'meet whom?' a clear sign that she too was thinking about the boy.

'I've no idea,' said Leopoldina, more decided, 'but I'm sure there must be a way.'

'Go and ring the bell of his apartment? Would we, you and I, ever stoop to that?'

'There must be a way of meeting him that would appear to have happened by chance.'

'For instance?'

'I can't think of anything right now.'

After a few minutes Henriette grumbled:

'Let him take the initiative. After all, he's a man.'

That was how Leopoldina knew for certain that Henriette too longed for the encounter, and made up her mind to speak, but quickly so that Henriette wouldn't interrupt her:

'One of these nights we go out, chatting loudly, making lots of noise in the elevator, so that he hears us. We have dinner in the restaurant next door. At ten-thirty we come back, but we don't go back up, we stay on the ground floor, in the foyer. When he comes out of the elevator, one of us fiddles with the key in the lock, as if we had come into the building that very second. Then we cross paths. It will be inevitable.'

'And then what? He'll say goodnight and carry on.'

'We could tell him we're his neighbours from the eighth floor, and that we like the tangos he plays on the accordion.'

'Would you dare, you, with your character?'

'I don't know. I don't think so. Not I.'

'Ah, you leave it up to me! I see. You had it all planned, your little scheme.'

She said no more. She didn't say if she agreed or if she didn't agree, but for a while she couldn't keep still. Leopoldina heard her rustling under the sheets and making a sort of snapping sound with her mouth, like someone savouring the last taste of a piece of candy.

Two days later, during lunch, Henriette said:

'Tonight we could eat at that restaurant next door.'

Her words made Leopoldina bold.

'No, not at that restaurant. I'm never at ease in such a noisy place.'

Henriette flared up:

'It was your idea, not mine!'

'Yes, but I've given it more thought, and actually we don't even need to go to the restaurant.'

At nine-thirty they switched off the lights, slammed a few doors, and the elevator seconded them in their efforts with its repertoire of squeaks and creaks. To wait, standing in the foyer until eleven, was sheer torture. Henriette seemed the most nervous of the two, sighing and making, every so often, a gesture as if to say something and immediately regretting it. Leopoldina instead stood quiet as a statue, but with her eyes wide open.

Henriette glanced at her wristwatch. 'Quarter past

eleven,' she whispered. Leopoldina, to indicate that this piece of information was unimportant, made no response. At eleven-thirty Henriette wanted to go back upstairs to their apartment, muttering that what they were doing was shameful, crouching in the shadows like two hussies. But Leopoldina remained motionless and silent, even though, judging by the look on her face, she seemed on the brink of despair.

At midnight, without asking for a second opinion, Henriette walked to the elevator and Leopoldina followed. As the elevator crossed the seventh floor, they heard the accordion. Henriette gave Leopoldina a furious look, but Leopoldina had her eyes cast down and pearls of sweat glistened all over her face. The accordion sounded very near, very distinct, as if the boy were playing it behind his apartment door. It must have been this that most fired Henriette's anger. Once again, she suffered an attack of asthma. She probably thought that the boy was doing it on purpose, to mock them. Leopoldina instead thought this: 'He's there, behind the door, ready to welcome us into his home.'

While she was getting undressed, blindly tearing off her clothes, Henriette abandoned her haughty manner and adopted a throaty and somewhat vulgar voice:

'You'll be pleased, I'm sure, with your wonderful plan. I don't know how, but he found out. He knew that we were waiting for him downstairs, like two courtesans. And he didn't come out. Tonight of all nights, he decided not to leave, just to humiliate us. All this time he was there, serenading us, simply to make fun of us, to laugh at us. Ah, but no one laughs at me, no sir, and certainly not that snot-nosed kid!'

Leopoldina was taking her clothes off with movements so weak and so unwilling that she seemed to be undressing for her deathbed. When at last she switched off the light, she heard Henriette's muffled voice coming from underneath the sheet that she had pulled over her head:

'First thing tomorrow I'll lodge a complaint at the office.'

She lodged no complaint. But every night, after dinner, she'd put on the gramophone, at full volume, the recording of a Wagner opera. The Nibelungian uproar or the Venusberg bacchanal must have made themselves heard not only throughout the entire building but also on Leandro Alem and in the faraway towers of Las Catalinas. If, meanwhile, he played his accordion, it was impossible to ascertain.

In the midst of the din, Leopoldina would beg:

'A little lower, please, Henriette!'

Henriette would stamp her foot on the floor.

'No! If he can deafen us with his accordion, so can I.'

She became sarcastic:

'Let him find out what music we really like. And if

he still doesn't know who we are, let him go and ask Wilson.'

What would Wilson tell him? *The Misses Wels, German or daughters of a German, I believe. Very aristocratic. They're not in the prime of their youth, but they're very beautiful, especially the eldest, Henriette.* What a pity that Wilson wouldn't be able to provide more details: that their grandfather had been a general of the Emperor Franz Josef, and that on their mother's side they were related to the Vizinzey, Hungarian noblemen, descendants of the Esterházy, the protectors of Haydn.

No doubt Wilson was also capable of saying to him: *Two old maids, rotten with pride, even though the youngest, Leopoldina, seems a more agreeable person; but she's under the other one's foot, and that one's a cavalry sergeant.* And it would have been nice, but seemingly impossible, if Wilson were to add: *Leopoldina never married because Henriette, always green with envy, used to frighten away all her beaus.* These thoughts were Leopoldina's, not Henriette's.

While Wagner's bellowings deafened the night, Leopoldina would go out on the balcony. She didn't wish to have a hand in Henriette's revenge. She'd go out on the balcony and say to herself that, just a few metres below, the boy would be feeling mortified, believing that she didn't like his tangos, imagining that she despised him. Perhaps the other night he'd had a good reason not to go out. He might have been ill. But even ill, he'd played the accordion to entice them to come and keep him company. And why not? What's wrong with two decent ladies paying a visit to a neighbour who's all alone and sick? Who, starting with the boy himself, would take them for a pair of loose women?

Then, one night, she felt she could take it no longer. She left the balcony and yelled so that Henriette would hear her over the Wagnerian uproar:

'Enough, for God's sake, enough Wagner! It's getting on my nerves! And with this hot weather! I'm about to go crazy!'

Henriette too must have been fed up with all those howling Valkyries and all those Götterdämmerungs, but must have found it hard to give in. Now, by pretending that she was complying with Leopoldina's request, she had found an opportunity of ridding herself of Wagner. But she wasn't willing to listen again to the accordion. She silenced Wagner and put on a record in which Dinu Lipatti tinkled some impromptus by Chopin.

And on the following night she pretended to be so deeply engrossed in a book that she didn't even notice the silence that surrounded them. Leopoldina refused to go out on the balcony. Something told her that this night would be decisive. She sat on the edge of a chair, as if ready to stand up at any minute, and waited.

Sure enough, at ten-thirty they received the message. It wasn't a tango, it was a waltz. My God, the *Blue*

Danube! The boy was playing the *Blue Danube*! He played it badly, haltingly. But for that very reason, the accordion seemed like a stammering voice, broken by emotion or by tears. The boy was asking their forgiveness. The boy wanted them to be reconciled. And in all humility, he had chosen the only music at his disposal that they weren't likely to refuse, even if he could only stammer it.

Leopoldina stood up, and with a hand to her throat as if to calm the pulsations of her blood, heard the first bars of the waltz. She was unable to control her own voice:

'Don't you realize? He knows who we are, and he's playing the *Blue Danube* for us. For us. He's always been playing for us. He knows us.'

Henriette hadn't stirred. She had stopped reading the book but she hadn't stirred—perhaps because of her pride—so as not to show any emotion. Leopoldina's reaction shook her. She seemed startled. She made a violent gesture, signalling to Leopoldina to lower her voice.

'He knows us? And from where do you suppose that he know us?'

'I've no idea. But he knows we've got Viennese blood and that's why he's playing the *Blue Danube*. It can't be a simple coincidence. I'm telling you, he knows us.'

She was so inflamed that Henriette stood up and held her by the arm.

'If he knows us it's because Wilson must have told him that on the eighth floor are these two women who live on their own, accompanied by an old servant who's half-deaf. Two rich women, in an apartment full of valuables.'

Leopoldina tore herself away.

'No. If he were a thief he wouldn't have waited this long to come rob us. That boy wants to be our friend.'

'Our friend? At his age it's not women friends he'd be after, it's mistresses.'

'Yes, all right. A mistress. I'm not that old, after all.'

For a moment, it seemed as if Henriette would become furious. But suddenly she let herself fall on a couch, knees apart, arms hanging loose, body dropped backwards.

'Leopoldina, have you lost your mind? What non-sense are you talking?'

'No nonsense. That boy wants to establish a friend-ship with us. At least with one of us.'

'And you know which one.'

'I'm the youngest, don't forget.'

'I wonder if you haven't gone utterly crazy.'

'Maybe. But this time you won't be able to prevent it.'

'Prevent what?'

'You know perfectly well, Henriette. You've done it all your life.'

All of a sudden they realized that the boy had

stopped playing the *Blue Danube* and that now there was silence. Leopoldina went and sat in an armchair, next to the entrance hall, and assumed a glacial air that Henriette had never seen her assume before.

'In a few minutes he'll be here, probably wearing a tuxedo.'

'Will you let him in?'

'Of course.'

'And if it isn't you he's coming to visit?'

'We'll see about that.'

Leopoldina straightened herself in her seat, Henriette did the same in hers. They glared at one another, as if in defiance. But the minutes went by and the bell didn't ring. And because it's uncomfortable to maintain for a long time an arrogant posture, they both put an end to their ocular duel, turning their heads in opposite directions and leaning their backs on the chairs' embroidered ovals.

When they heard the slamming door, the elevator shaking, the habitual noises indicating that the boy was leaving, Leopoldina didn't move but Henriette burst out laughing.

'Your beau can't make up his mind. He's obviously a shy one.'

Without deigning to answer, Leopoldina went to lie down on the bed, fully dressed. After a while, Henriette came into the room. As the dining-room clock struck twelve, Henriette's voice issued from the darkness of the bedroom. It was a soft voice, it seemed to show concern.

'I didn't mean to offend you. But you won't deny that the young man's behaviour is pretty odd.'

Leopoldina didn't answer. And so that Henriette wouldn't think she was asleep, she switched on the lamp by the bed, looked at the time on the clock on the night-table, and turned the lamp off again. She still hadn't undressed.

Afterwards Henriette insisted:

'Don't get your hopes too high. That kind of man is not for us.'

Once again, Leopoldina didn't answer.

During the following day Leopoldina didn't utter a single word. She wore a wounded expression on her face and a look of violence in her eyes. In the afternoon, Wilson arrived with the news: the seventh-floor tenant had moved out, he had no idea where.

'Now you'll be able to sleep in peace. The danger is past.'

And he added a few unexpected words, coming as they did from such a coarse individual:

'*Swallows of a single summer ...*'

That night, Leopoldina, still not saying a word, still mortally wounded, walked out on the balcony, softly, as if she were levitating. Holding herself very upright, she stared into the distance at the lights of the dockyards, and further away, at the river of zinc glittering in the moonlight. Henriette was watching her from indoors. Then she left the book she was reading (which she hadn't even opened) and went outside to stand next to her sister. Elbow to elbow, stiff-backed and staring straight ahead, the Misses Wels would have seemed, to a casual observer, two princesses from some Northern country watching, from the balcony of their palace, a military parade.

After a quarter of an hour, Leopoldina said:

'Have you noticed, Henriette? No one lives across the road. They're nothing but transients on the other side of the Avenida Leandro Alem.'

'How true,' Henriette answered. 'I hadn't noticed.'

THE REDEMPTION OF THE CANNIBAL WOMAN

The moment she stepped out onto the stage she saw him sitting in the front row. Something drew her to the figure of the young man who seemed even younger among the old greybeards. Very blond, lots of curly hair, the face of an English cabin-boy with still-innocent features, a decent blue suit, white shirt with an open collar turned over the lapels, he seemed to her the foreign type, a tourist, and very handsome, in spite of a somewhat gangling physique as if he were still suffering from the aftershocks of growing up.

But what puzzled her most was the manner in which this Englishman seemed to be watching the show: legs stretched out and crossed at the ankles, body sunk into the seat, hands dug flat into the trouser pockets, head turned to one side, a posture that pumped up his shoulder-pads and obliterated his neck. And since, to make things worse, he was chewing something (a piece of candy, she imagined) with a full mouth and a languid working of the jawbones, she had the impression of a man displaying either indolence or a somewhat conceited boredom.

Coral Queen quickly realized that the blond was not just another member of the audience. That he wasn't even truly *part* of the audience. He was following the show against his will. To say the least, he was watching her as if someone had sent him to observe her and describe later what he had seen, and the task had become a nuisance. He watched her as if he had come to examine her and was already fed up with, or resigned to the job of inspecting chorus girls. Because a man who watches a woman while he chews candy and slouches in that manner has something calculating, scornful, something of a judge, an overseer, even a hangman.

A producer, she thought. A producer who had come to the Cosmopolitan looking for merchandise for his business and had found nothing satisfactory, or maybe he put on the appearance of being a tough customer in order to be able to haggle over the price later on. Or rather a devoted fan. A devoted fan who feels compelled to watch what he's watched thousands of times and knows by heart, and whose only pleasure is the sweetness of the candy with which he keeps up appearances.

In short: Coral Queen guessed that the blond had landed at the Cosmopolitan for reasons best known to himself, reasons kept secret for the time being but which in any case were different from those of the rest of the audience.

She did her number and the audience did theirs.

Coral Queen measured 1.85 metres in her stockinged feet. With her shoes on, the high heels lifted her up to over 1.90. She stuck a feather in her hair and the feather scraped the grill on the ceiling. Seen from the stalls, she looked like a monument set on a generous pedestal.

In those days, the municipal regulations allowed chorus girls a nakedness equivalent nowadays to that of a bundled-up Eskimo. Arms and legs uncovered, a neckline barely lower than that of any upper-class young lady, absence of girdle and bra, and that was it. Dressed in that fashion, Coral Queen gave the unequivocal impression of being a pugilist in drag. One admired her stature, one admired her dry muscled extremities and her hefty body, one stared her in the face, and without meaning to be unkind one became convinced that Coral Queen had in the past been a boxer. The large bulge at breast level didn't dispel the notion that, rather than a pair of female breasts, these looked like the knees of a squatting fat man, jutting, who knows how, from either side of the sternum. Such a bosom, too voluminous and stiff not to be false, with the mouthpiece of a horn in the place of each nipple, did nothing but proclaim to the world that all this was only a colossal charade.

And to top it all, the face. Not even the most conceited of men would find amiss a nose such as Coral Queen's nose, which on a male promised other natural enormities, or that teeth-grinding jaw that seemed on the point of hurling insults at whoever tried anything funny. And as if all this were not enough, she made her face up in a sort of frenzy, so that she ended up with more features than required, as if she wore two faces, one overlapping the other, and both cumbersome. Finally, an enormous carrot-coloured mane, barbed with coils, sat perched on her head, somewhat off-centre, like an angry wig.

Enticed by such lack of decent appearance, the public suspected that the gargantuan chorus girl was of a trumped-up sex. A transvestite, they would declare. And as transvestites might kick up their heels at secret orgies, but would never parade openly on stage, the public, seeing Coral Queen, would gasp with a sudden asthmatic wheeze and clutch their seats so as not to fall backwards in astonishment.

Let it be understood that this public was not made up of innocent little angels. One had only to see the way they cheered the chorus girls: with stamping feet, whistles, cheeky cackles, vulgar expletives and the occasional emission of wind, not to mention the pranks they played on one another as they smoked without taking off their hats, or the rivulets of urine that ran down the sloping floor between the surprised feet of those in front. If they happened to applaud, their applause sounded anything but laudatory, contradicted by the verbal and onomatopoeic accompaniment.

Something curious: the acts that did not offend decency—for instance, a couple of supposedly gypsy dancers, a juggler or a folk singer, however imbecile— would garner plaudits. Of course, in those days sex was a gimmick invented by women for their exclusive benefit, or against women for their exclusive prejudice, and the Cosmopolitan's customers, so as to show that they, so manly, were not to be fooled by the gimmick, pretended to make fun of the crudely sexual performances and reserved their encomium for those acts that were not. This is also the reason for the once deeply rooted and today neglected masculine contempt of erotic exhibitionism. Those who think of a brothel as rowdy and shameless never visited one.

But faced with Coral Queen, the public neither applauded nor hooted, as if they were incapable of knowing what to do with a transvestite. What they all agreed on was that the transvestite was obviously unhappy with his fate. To begin with, he was not at all effeminate, if one were to judge him by his face, his body and his manners. And he seemed a decent enough person. No doubt he took part in this cross-dressing against his will, to earn a living. Anyone could guess he was itching to plough a fist into the first person to make fun of him. So the spectators felt hardly inclined to be boisterous, and became instead rather sullen and hushed. They gazed on Coral Queen much like children witnessing a birth and having no idea what it was all about. Perhaps in the depth of their astonishment lay terror, the almost religious fascination that since ancient times simple people have always felt in the presence of those who, in reality or in fiction, change from one sex into the other, or share both simultaneously.

The manager of the Cosmopolitan fostered their fear by introducing Coral Queen as 'The Cannibal Woman,' and adding another untruth: 'Recently arrived from the Caribbean.'

Dressed in a tumult of straw, feathers and beads, face painted to the point of vertigo, Coral Queen came on stage at a gallop, like something in search of food. Not finding it, she threw a tantrum, put on the face of an upset man-eater, kicked a few times high into the air, slapped her hands around, gave her feathers a shake, rattled the totemic beads, and in the midst of the musical din, made her way to the front of the stage.

The greybeards in the first row would huddle together in fright. She would look them over, one by one, as if to choose the tastiest one, walking from one end of the stage to the other without taking her eyes off them, throwing ferocious grimaces in their direction; then she'd stop suddenly and move her breasts as if the fat man had suddenly been overcome by an epileptic fit. More than one fool would look down to see if the transvestite's stuffing had come loose. Coral Queen would turn round, wiggle her buttocks, and turn again, go back to the famished expression and the hungry contortions, and finally two dancers would approach her cautiously, take her by the hands, and carry her backstage, like trainers carrying away a wild beast to its cage, or rather, like two *couturiers* exiting with their dressmaker's dummy, offended because no one had bought their nice new outfit.

The public refrained even from signalling its presence. While the Cannibal Woman made gestures indicative of her intentions to eat, the men sat still as corpses into which it would be futile to sink one's teeth. And when she'd leave with an empty belly, they let her go in the midst of a heartfelt relief that would quickly intensify with the appearance of the chorus girls of ascertained sex.

But that night there was a change. While pacing the stage, Coral Queen lavished on the Englishman her greedy looks and savage gnashing of teeth. He, without disturbing his body's indifferent pose, followed her with quicksilver eyes and vigorous acceleration of the jaws. Afterwards, as she retired between the two *couturiers*, Coral Queen turned and looked at him once more. And then, unexpectedly, someone applauded. But not a mock applause: a perfectly clean and straightforward applause. It was the cabin-boy who was applauding. The others seemed to realize that their taboo bore no relevance to the transvestite who was after all a man, and that they could clap without imperilling their honour. Behind Coral Queen's back there broke out a thunderous clapping such as no chorus girl had ever received, and least of all this one.

Backstage ran a quiver of surprise. This was the first time something like this had happened. And to whom? To that butch-looking Coral Queen. It became known that the initiative had come from a spectator in the front row. They'd seek him out later; right now, the women's scorn reared its front hooves. 'Her Majesty's got a visitor tonight,' they said, 'and a cute one, too. Well, you better believe it, some men like them ugly.' But no one made a comment to her face, partly because they were well aware of her prickly character, and partly so as not to give her the opportunity of showing off.

In the dressing-room shared with two other stars, in the midst of a mess of clothes and the stench of cosmetics and sweat, Coral Queen sat down and for a while observed herself motionless in the mirror, as if she were a stranger, breathing heavily like someone who has just come out of a shouting match. It wasn't only the jig she had just finished dancing on stage that was making her gasp. It was also the emotion.

Before her second number she watched him from the wings. Now the blond young man, his legs still stretched out, had his eyes shut. He didn't even open them for the act entitled 'All Bets on Seven.' Nor did he open them when Cresencio Leanes, a.k.a. Ling-Wu-Chang, began to display his magic tricks. It seemed as if the show had become, for the cabin-boy, nothing more than a nuisance. But he wasn't asleep. He kept on chewing candy after candy, and in order to dig those candies out of his pocket, to take the wrapper calmly off and pop the candy in his mouth, he'd pull his hands out from the depths of his trouser pockets, and then put them back in again as if his hands were a pair of duelling-pistols. And not even the audience's cackling laughter as the first comedian delivered his ancient jokes altered his great indifference or scorn.

But as soon as Coral Queen reappeared on stage, the devoted fan seemed to wake up. And without changing his apathetic and cocky position, he opened his eyes and in each eye a certain shine appeared; he uncrossed and again crossed his legs at the ankles as if settling into a more comfortable position, and the jaws crunched the candy with renewed energy. Coral Queen no longer doubted it: the blond young man was here for her. And earlier, he had clapped simply to let her know.

He had come for her. *And with what intention?* she asked herself. Would he simply pick her up like a young and dapper Cossack? She'd be satisfied with just that. At last a man who wasn't old or ugly. But she couldn't stop herself from wondering. Perhaps he'd come to take her with him. Where? To another theatre, to a dancehall? No doubt that theatre would have a higher standard than this moth-ridden Cosmopolitan. No doubt the dancehall would be a luxurious affair and not some dive in the slums. Because the Englishman himself was of a different class, a luxury item amidst the riff-raff and the decrepit audience. Maybe the cabin-boy was the manager of an international circus, maybe he was in search of outlandish acts and the Cannibal Woman was exactly what he was looking for. Youth, in an Englishman, is no obstacle to power. But these thoughts allowed Coral Queen to avoid thinking about something else, something so wonderful that it frightened her. And yet that something slid in between her other thoughts like the sound of a bell in the midst of a conversation.

She tried harder than ever before. Never had she appeared as tall, as carnivorous and pugilistic as that night. It seemed as if at any given moment she'd jump into the audience and devour one of the open-mouthed dummies who were watching her in terror. She didn't look at the blond young man except in a passing glance. A shyness or modesty, directed exclusively towards him, or perhaps the wish that no one realize what was taking place, prevented her from looking at him face to face. But even then she managed to notice that he had his eyes tied up in an all-attentive knot, and that across the curving lips was spreading the smile of a man who knows his business. She also saw the wrappers lying around him on the floor, and in that shower of what looked like blobs of spittle, Coral Queen recognized the sign of a certain bravado or pride, as if the little Englishman were bragging of sullying himself at the Cosmopolitan, between the whores on stage and the scum in the audience. All, except her. On her he continued to bestow that concentrated interest that made him almost cross-eyed in his vigilance, that tenuous smile that meant he was well aware of what was going on. And when Coral Queen made her exit, the solitary applause broke out again, and the fools in the audience echoed it with their own.

During the intermission, Coral Queen was seen peeping at the audience through the gap in the curtains, thereby confirming the fact that this monstrosity indeed had her admirers, and that one of them was that very delectable young man seated in the front row. When they saw her return to her dressing-room with a beatific look, taking small steps as if she were treading on cobblestones, rather like a chorus girl or even like a chorus boy, they felt their blood boil because of the unfairness of fate, and no longer bothered to hide their ironic or spiteful gossip.

Their hostility didn't touch her. What she had seen through the gap in the curtains had convinced her that the cabin-boy would carry her away with him. During the intermissions, the spectators walked out into the lobby to stretch their legs and into the john to relieve their bladders. But the blond man's legs were already stretched out, and he had such nice manners that he didn't pee except at home. He remained in his seat, now sitting upright, head straight, neck strong and elbows and knees apart, like a gentleman in an armchair ready to have his picture taken.

Coral Queen was able to examine him from head to toe because the house was now lit up and she was hidden behind the curtains. At first she was startled: he had his eyes fixed exactly on the gap through which she was looking out, as if he were able to see through the cloth and knew that she was there, spying on him. But immediately those very same eyes calmed her fears. The colour of mercury, they seemed fluorescent with the radiant and peaceful aspect of a full moon in a summer sky. *That is what angels must look like,* she thought. Further down, the mouth, chewing on the endless candy, appeared to be mimicking a movement of silent words, like someone who, without uttering a single sound, deliberately exaggerates the pantomime of the lips for someone else to grasp a message at a distance. Coral Queen grasped it: she wasn't certain of what the text said, but she understood that the message promised her happiness.

And the blond young man was handsome: it was as simple as that. His features were small and delicate but forceful, taut as if a spring held them together from inside. His skin was like felt, his chin determined, the neck as wide as the face and with a prominent Adam's apple, a detail that in his case lent him a certain voluptuousness. His entire appearance radiated self-confidence and quiet strength, a kind of animal vigour that seemed to make him oblivious to his surroundings. *With a man like that,* Coral Queen thought, *I could go anywhere in the world.*

Convinced that he was watching her, she signalled to him that he was to wait for her after the show. Incredibly, the young man responded with a quick nod and a spark in his mercury eyes. For Coral Queen, there and then, life began to turn in the whirlpools of witchcraft. Or perhaps it was God Himself who sent her this angel. That is why she returned to her dressing-room with a mystic look on her face and a tiptoeing step, already indifferent to the miseries of the Cosmopolitan as one might be indifferent to a dirty towel left abandoned in the room of one's hotel.

For her third and final act, she always chose to perform the pantomime of a massacre. Spurred on by the caterwaul of the small orchestra, she would step out on stage with the entire troop of chorus boys dressed up, as she was, in cannibal outfits; they would twist around for a few seconds, and then Coral Queen, doing a dance step that rather resembled the kicking of a tin, would knock down one by one the flighty dancers who were trying to look terribly savage, and would at last be the only one left standing, arms stretched upwards, the long legs wide apart and the feathers grazing the ceiling, in the midst of the musical din. Taking advantage of the applause, she glanced at the blond young man and, filled with sudden courage, she winked at him. He lifted a candy holding it between his thumb and index finger, showed it to her quite openly, and then put it in his mouth, as if the candy were a sign to be deciphered as it was being swallowed. Then Coral Queen knew that God was protecting her, that God had sent her the benediction of this man. As an act of thanks, she added to the massacre an apotheosis of awkward gestures and contortions. This time the public didn't wait for anyone to spur them on: the ovation came all on its own.

In the shows put on in that miserable little theatre there was no final curtain. The last act was played out with the curtain down and exclusively for spectators in the know. Chorus girls and other *artistes* (except those who were married and liked to make a big display of their faithfulness) descended from the stage in single file, already dressed in their civilian clothes, and walked through the house out into the lobby without looking at anyone, very much in a hurry not to miss the last late-night streetcar. A remnant of the audience watched the parade, silent as soldiers during a forced conscription. A few customers followed the performers, completely hooked; others waited for them in the bar of the lobby. And from there they'd leave a while later, to become de facto engaged in some neighbouring hotel or—a fortunate few—in a bachelor's den, if they didn't first wander through the dockside nightclubs where more than one of the girls had a second job.

Coral Queen hung around the bar in the lobby. She appeared last, once the stragglers had become drunk on gin and felt confident. Every night she would have the same thought: *Maybe tonight I'll be lucky.* She never was. The men avoided her with enthusiasm. As soon as that mistaken semblance of a woman entered the lobby, those who had a date would devote themselves to earnest conversations, and those who were on their own would suffer from strained necks aimed in the opposite direction, as if Coral Queen had been a bully spoiling for a fight, and no one was feeling up to rousing her temper. The only ones who dared were the Russkies. But she hated the Russkies who, apart from anything else, were scarce.

They were known as the Russkies because they looked Russian, Ukranian, Polish or somewhere in that area. They were squarish individuals, sturdy as scaffolding, almost invariably topped with a bald skull, flat nose, an obscenely foreign accent, well past middle-age and with the look of a police sergeant who before asking questions lets it be known that the answer had better be yes. Dressed with funereal severity, perfumed, and some even manicured, each the proud owner of a ring and black homburg, they deceived no one: anyone could sniff from miles away the turpentine stench of some secret and infamous crime.

If there happened to be one of these in the lobby, Coral Queen knew that tonight she wouldn't have her share of the luck she so desired, but that at least she wouldn't have to sleep alone. Certainly not alone: going to bed with a Russkie was like going to bed with twenty, each one bolder than the rest.

Almost immediately she'd have him at her beck and call, as he'd strip her down to the bare skin with his policeman's eyes. First they'd chat ceremoniously. When she wanted to, Coral Queen could speak with flawless grammar. She was capable of taking on the tone of a matron at a wake and saying to the Slav:

'I'm told that communists advocate free love. Is it true, or is it merely a slur?'

The Russkie, his throat clogged with seriousness, would answer:

'It's the truth, but I myself am all for marriage.'

The matron would sigh:

'I quite agree. If I haven't yet tied the knot it's because the theatre is my religion.'

The Russkie would growl with an accent:

'Of course.'

And while the secret policeman's eyes would scrutinize Coral Queen's breasts as if to force them to confess that they were fake, she'd respond with smiles that declared her to be guilty, and anyone watching them was likely to believe that, with the grimaces and the questioning of the cleavage, the two were trying to hide from the world the real subject of their conversation.

Until the Muscovite's hand would snake like a reptile towards the hand of Coral Queen and suddenly bite it. Then the two would abandon the lobby and head off towards Coral Queen's room, deep in the hollow of a downtown boarding-house.

In bed, the twenty Russkies competed against each other to turn a normally simple task into a complicated struggle. Unbelievable, all that can be done with only a few elements! To be the object of such vehemence ultimately succeeded in making Coral Queen feel flattered. And having always been a grateful woman, she backed each of the twenty Russkies without neglecting a single one.

At daybreak, the Russkie, now reduced to a single individual, would leave as if pushing a dead elephant, and she would doze off in a cataleptic quicksand in that room impregnated with the stench of dried wallpaper glue and rotten sandalwood. When on the following afternoon she'd return to her senses, the stench, and the memory of that which out of gratitude she'd perpetrated for the Russkie on the previous night, would make her furious. She'd guess that these foreigners sought her out because for them the ideal woman would be another man, but a man who had between the legs that which only women have—and she fit the picture perfectly. They knew that in bed she'd behave like a man and even better, with a great sense of initiative and mutual assistance, and not as (they imagined) most women did, like a magician's helper, reaching him his top hat and then waiting to see what he'll pull out of it. She instead brought to the business of bedding a woman's capital and a man's labours.

Every time it happened, she swore not to allow herself ever again to get entangled with a Russkie. But when there were no Cossacks to be seen in the lobby, she mournfully regretted their absence. On such occasions, while the other tramps and even one of the nancy boys scored the best candidates, she'd pull on the face of a spinster who by mistake has entered the men's room and who, while looking for the exit, hides her embarrassment under a mask of scorn, lifts a nose injured by the odours and looks straight ahead in order not to see so many open flies. Immediately she'd leave the lobby without ordering a drink, she'd walk up Veinticinco de Mayo along the gawking corridor of nightclubs that forbid entry to single women, she'd head towards the boarding-house, and once in her room, mix herself a glass of anything and then get into bed.

But before falling asleep she'd review her dream: one night a stranger who had once caught sight of her would come and rescue her from the Cosmopolitan, from the Russkies, from the furnished room, from the dockyard neighbourhoods, from herself, from Coral Queen, from the Cannibal Woman. The stranger would take her with him to another place where she'd be happy.

Now that impossible dream seemed about to become reality. Perhaps the young Englishman was the stranger who had seen her once and who would take her away, an angel who had come to save her from growing old among the riff-raff of Veinticinco de Mayo. *Don't you believe it,* she told herself. *Be content if the blond young man approaches you in the lobby and offers you a drink.* She'd be content with just that. She'd be content if the blond young man were to propose a fleeting fornication and in bed made her undergo the same rigours as the Russkies or other exercises even more outrageous. Finally, she'd be content even if at the last moment the Englishman were to change his mind and refuse to touch her with his little finger. All she wanted was this: to leave the lobby, just for one night, on the arm of a handsome young man, to rub it into the noses of all those cows and pansies who were always making fun of her, to show them all that Coral Queen was not an odd dish eaten only by those with an ailing palate.

Suddenly she decided that if the blond young man were to offer her a contract with another theatre, with a dancehall or a circus, she'd accept on the spot, even if the theatre were worse than the Cosmopolitan, even if the dancehall were a brothel and the circus a flea-pit. Her one and only condition: that the Englishman agree to become hers.

She dressed in a hurry. The two colleagues with whom she shared the dressing-room watched her from the corners of their eyes. They said nothing so as not to be the first to give in, but she could sniff their malodorous spite. While she put on enough make-up to cover four separate faces, she hummed between her teeth, and as she was leaving she spat out:

'See you tomorrow, dolls. Tonight I've got a heavy date.'

The envious bitches didn't even bother to answer.

She was the first to climb down from the stage, leading the single exiting file; contrary to her habit, she looked at the customers one by one. The young Englishman was nowhere to be seen. She couldn't believe that he'd left without waiting for her. *He must be waiting out in the street,* she thought. She did, however, see a Russkie who observed her with severity, like a pimp looking at a whore who had run away from the brothel. She paid no attention to him and walked towards the door. Behind her, the chorus girls followed her in a stampede to see whether there was or wasn't justice in this world.

Out on the street what she saw almost knocked her over. She saw the car. She saw an immense jewel, a marvel, a brand-new machinery, resplendent in chrome and nickel, parked by the curb on the other side. It was an open sedan the colour of mother-of-pearl, with the hood down, the spikes of the wheels painted white and with a huge windshield that lent it a certain bond of blood with a sports plane. The sedan sat on the cobbles like an exotic fowl, a costly animal, a bird of paradise, and the running motor provoked in it impatient tremors: the bird was preparing to take flight. Sitting at the steering-wheel, wearing an unexpected chequered cap down to the ears, the blond young man had his face turned towards the theatre lobby and was crunching the one-thousandth piece of candy, now faster and more energetically than before, appearing to share the car's tremor, as well as its impatience.

As soon as Coral Queen stepped out, the blond man, without interrupting the mastication, clutched the wheel as if threatening someone, and looked at the Cannibal Woman with such arrogance in his quicksilver eyes that she, from where she was standing, understood that the boy was giving her an order that she had at some other time not obeyed and that he now repeated as an ultimatum, determined not to allow her another disobedience. Intimidated by that tacit threat, overcoming any scruple she might have had, throwing aside the habitual fuss and circumlocutions, she crossed the street and climbed into the sedan, whose door the Englishman opened while constantly keeping an eye on Coral Queen's every move as if to dismantle her slightest hesitation. As soon as she sat back in the soft sweet-smelling leather seat, the car set off. A kind of giddiness forced her to turn her head and look back towards the Cosmopolitan: standing on the curb, the girls and one of the nancy boys were watching her, each with the expression of someone who had just received in the face the filth of an incomprehensible insult. She couldn't help it. The double mouth produced a double triumphant smile and her left hand performed in the air a gesture of goodbye that looked rather like the showing of a stiff middle finger. Then she turned round and looked ahead.

The car drove down Veinticinco de Mayo southwards, perhaps with no other purpose than to allow Coral Queen to bid adieu, forever, to that miserable neighbourhood. In any case, the young Englishman drove the car down that horrible street at walking speed. Maybe he did it to allow Coral Queen to savour her victory. She interpreted it in two ways: as a definitive leavetaking and as a revenge. Fully in possession of her role, she stiffened herself into the posture of a princess reviewing the colours.

It was Saturday, it was summer. The nightclubs aired their music, a deadened rumbling like the scraping of the pavement. There were people on the sidewalks. Groups of pilgrims went from door to door as if asking after a long-lost relative. Others stood waiting for them in the doorways to let them know that they might be able to find him inside. Gangs of sailors were displaying all the fervours of a national holiday. At the corners, young vacant men were gradually growing old enough to enter the dives. Tattered old men, sleepwalking old women, crouched at the mouth of long dark corridors, dozed with their eyes wide open. And even though in those years today's neon signs were unknown, one could sense, just like now, that atmosphere of preparations made the day before, the guarded or cheeky nervousness that always runs from nightclub to nightclub, as if in all, simultaneously, a guest of honour is being expected, a guest of honour who will never arrive.

While the car drove down that disreputable street, those in search of a relative stopped to see her pass and then kept on studying her with a worried look, as if they suspected that their relative was being spirited away in her car. The men in the doorways, the sailors on leave, the incubating young men, all took on the sombre airs of someone who sees his rival approaching and cannot decide between courage and cowardice. A recalcitrant courtesan stopped and stared at the car, and then at its occupants, as if trying to discover what the swindle was. A drunk greeted Coral Queen in the drunks' Esperanto; a stray kid bestowed upon them, either on Coral Queen or on the car, the tender gestures with which one celebrates, at that age, a passing train; a furtive streetwalker stabbed Coral Queen with piercing eyes that accused her of some crime or were a call for help. The old men and women observed Coral Queen and her blond young man with the surprised cataractic pupils with which one watches a house on fire. And from the depths of the Turkish or Arab rummage shops, the seedy hotels that let rooms by the hour, the burrowing boarding-houses, more than one sleepless eye sparkled, as the car went by, with a double sheen of curiosity and astonishment. Even the cuckolded tangos dribbling out onto the street from within the darkness of the dancehalls, even the adulterous boleros and sensual marimbas, all seemed to stop for a moment at the sight of Coral Queen taking flight with the angel, and then seemed to sing at her back their melancholic or provocative farewells of separation and abandonment.

Coral Queen, without shifting her posture, kept glimpsing from the corner of her eyes all that fury, that consternation, that sadness with which the deathly neighbourhood bid her goodbye. Then all her doubts vanished: the blond man was taking her away forever, and Veinticinco de Mayo, with the clairvoyance bestowed upon it by a life of crime, had guessed as much. She felt the urge, or rather the obligation to cry a little, because after all, saying goodbye, even if it is to a life of misery, is painful if one has given it all the best years of one's youth. But she was afraid that her tears might not be to the blond man's liking, so she opted instead for a sigh that would suffice for the neighbourhood to know that Coral Queen was leaving without ill feelings, and even with a certain nostalgia for the many difficulties they had overcome together.

The car reached Avenida Corrientes, turned left, raced down the steep descent, turned again and drove up Leandro Alem northwards, now at full speed. They crossed Retiro, entered the darkness of Avenida Alvear and coasted the gardens of Palermo.

With the excuse of fixing up her mane dishevelled by the speeding wind, every so often Coral Queen turned her head and surreptitiously glanced at the Englishman. He pretended not to notice, apparently concentrating on driving the car. His profile was as perfect as his full face. He had long, thin, very white hands, hairless. The cap made him look older. He smelled of vanilla, maraschino cherries and hard candy. And he never stopped chewing.

Who knows how another woman would have reacted. Some fools might have been fussy, might have asked the blond young man: 'Excuse my being inquisitive, but where are you taking me?' And would have spoilt everything. Coral Queen understood that she was to behave as if she were already aware of the boy's intentions, or at least as if she were agreeable beforehand and willing to obey. And yet, she would have liked him to have said even one word, make any kind of small talk. 'Are you called Queen because Queen is your name, or because you're so regal?' 'I didn't much like the show at the Cosmopolitan, with one exception: you. You are a true *artiste.*' 'Lovely evening, isn't it?' 'Do you enjoy travelling by car?' 'Would you care for a candy?' But the silent boy remained silent. Maybe he was a mute.

But his silence was not a mute's silence. Nor was it the silence of someone in a huff. The Englishman was chewing away with evident satisfaction, looking phlegmatic and of excellent digestion, and had the peaceful appearance of a man taking pleasure in his job. One could hardly suppose that he was shy. He had been far from shy when he had steered the Cannibal Woman away from the Cosmopolitan. Nor did he seem scornful. Rather, there was in his attitude the assuredness and ease of a professional doing his thing, a thing he knows by heart and about which he needs to make no fuss.

Coral Queen accepted his manners. Because there also was the story of the stranger who knew all about her, that fantasy she had concocted in the loneliness of her big room. Indeed, the blond young man appeared to know who she was and for that reason avoided all introductions or any other utterances. He was driving her wherever it was he had to drive her without making a great show of it. And the journey helped Coral Queen air herself out, get rid of the stench of misery. One cannot cross, all of a sudden, from a world inhabited by whores and hoodlums to the world of motorized angels. Coral Queen understood as much, and in order to disintoxicate herself all the faster she breathed in deep gulps of air. But she asked no questions, because questions might upset the delicate clockwork. A single word too many, a misplaced gesture, and she'd wake up again in the room on Viamonte, next to yet another Russkie.

The car climbed up a slope, entered a neighbourhood of tree-lined streets and mansions protected by railings and deep gardens. At this time of night and in a neighbourhood like this there was not a living soul to be seen. They scuttled down an alley narrow as a tunnel dug out among the foliage. Every so often the tunnel crossed another, and at the crossing shone, high up, a street-lamp whose light, yellow and cloudy, lit a snippet of the lace-patterned dome. Right and left there continued the parade of iron gates, of tenebrous parks, of sleeping houses with a small light lit on one side as if protecting the houses' sleep. There were no cars except those that, from time to time, appeared heaped like junk next to the curb. Only the young man's car drove on. Its headlights pierced the shadows like the flashlight of a thief, and the motor repeated a cautious puffing. The tires, flattening a dry leaf, provoked an alarmed whisper. And there was no moon.

Then the car stopped, the puffing ceased and the lights were extinguished. The blond young man opened the door and got out. What could Coral Queen do except follow him? They were in front of one of the many palatial villas. She saw two great iron gates, various metres high and wide, crowned by an arch-shaped creeper. Behind it she saw a brick-dust path, a garden, a statue, a square and grey shape that seemed suspended in mid-air, she saw the balustrades of the balconies, the columns of the portico, the windows with stern shutters. Two lamps were lit at each of the house's front corners and allowed one to make out all the sumptuous details.

The blond man jangled his keys and opened one of the gates. Then he turned towards Coral Queen, looked at her and once again signalled an order. She didn't resist. But as soon as she had crossed that mysterious threshold, she stopped and waited. The young man closed the gate, walked towards the house, never bothered to check whether Coral Queen was following him or not. Nor was it necessary: the small noise of her shoes on the brick dust let him know that she was close behind. What the noise didn't reveal was that her heart was pounding hard and that entering a house like this one gave her the shivers, as if she were approaching a dreadful revelation. Her legs were trembling, her high heels were twisting as if made out of rubber.

The inside of the palace stunned her. For a moment she was unable to see anything, or nothing in particular, and yet her eyes took everything in. I mean that at a single glance and in a single intake of breath she knew that she had arrived at a place where all the riches in the world were hoarded, all the beauty and luxury that time can accumulate in a single house. No human being, however assiduous, is able to amass such opulence. It is Humanity itself that throughout the years had chosen this piece of furniture, then that other one, collecting one by one all these various objects, some miniscule, others enormous, then storing them in a house so as not to allow them to be lost.

Everything was motionless, luminous and orderly as in a painting. Everything was like a vast decor set out and ready for the arrival of the actors. But the decor had been erected so that the actors, beautiful and well-dressed, might move around like marquises and speak complicated sentences in a language understood only by the rich. No one could speak here in the same way one spoke in the street. Nor could one move here in the same way one moved in other places. Here special gestures were required, a difficult vocabulary. Even feelings would be different here. No tantrums, no envy, no betrayals, no stabbings in the back as at the Cosmopolitan. And certainly not the lust of the Russkies. Here men and women would fall in love, but as in the movies. Sometimes they'd suffer, but only because of the death of a loved one, never because the loved one had left them for someone else with more money. In a house like this hunger never entered, nor the sicknesses that kill the poor. One had to be very well-off, very refined, very well-mannered, have travelled to Europe, have jewellery, furs, a car, to be admitted into this mansion. But if that was the case, why had they let her in? Did they or didn't they know that she was Coral Queen, chorus girl from the Cosmopolitan, the Cannibal Woman, the Cossacks' prey? Wouldn't they see the circus colours painted on her face? Wouldn't they see the red silk dress, the sealing-wax mane, the heavy tin bracelets? Might this not be a mistake? Just in case, she improvised for herself a sudden decency; that is to say that, rather than puff herself up like the matron to whom one presents one's condolences at a wake, she put on a haughty, almost offended face, even though her legs wouldn't stop trembling.

The Englishman leading, she following, they crossed

an antechamber, a large hall, another, climbed an enormous staircase, arrived at a sort of theatre-box. Coral Queen felt that the furniture, the tremendous vases, the paintings were watching her. She never lifted her eyes from the carpets. She walked on tiptoe, because her heels insisted on bending sideways. She exaggerated, just in case, the offended expression, with the result that it appeared as if the matron were being dragged, against her will, to pay her respects to someone on his deathbed. The only liberty she allowed herself to take was this: to slide, along the banister, an outstretched finger on which a nail shone like a drop of dried blood. If she were to trip, she hoped that this finger would save her from a fall.

The cabin-boy stopped in front of a heavily carved door, knocked gently several times, and without waiting for an answer—if there was one, Coral Queen never heard it—he opened the door and immediately, with his hand still on the handle, stepped to one side and gave her one of his implacably commanding looks. In that split second Coral Queen realized that the Englishman was simply someone else's messenger. And now she was to appear in front of that someone. Then her mind went blank. Without a single thought, she walked in. Later she'd realize that the blond man had shut the door behind her, leaving her alone with the someone else, thereby formalizing the opinion that the blond man was nothing but an intermediary, a chauffeur, a servant.

But Coral Queen was too busy with her own fright to think much about the Englishman. For a while she was overcome by a blindness to details. She saw nothing but heaps of objects. She saw what she knew were arm-chairs, books, pictures, statuettes, china, gold, silver, marble, ivory and crystal, but had one asked her what one thing or another actually was, she would have been unable to answer. Amidst the quiet chaos she recognized, like a familiar face or a welcoming gesture, a bouquet of tea roses. The ochre light of a lamp floated faintly in mid-air and the whole room seemed enveloped in mist, in smoke, in the folds of a mosquito-net. She could smell several intermingled fragrances. The strict tic-toc of a clock could be heard, invisible and near. A great silence pervaded the room.

Until the man moved, until the wine-coloured stain began to emerge from the intricate furnishings, Coral Queen was unaware that she was not alone. When she realized that the moment had come to face the presence of the other, her breath stuck in her throat. The man was drifting towards her through the ochre mist, through the undergrowth of furniture. He was advancing in a crooked line, slowly, as if changing direction at every other step. Finally he placed himself barely two feet away from Coral Queen. At that very moment, she had no head for trivialities. But later she would realize that the other was a short and thinnish man, with a very white face, very smooth and as if stretched and starched and ironed, a composite face on which someone had glued together the heterogeneous features of several men: egg-shaped eyes, with no eyelids or lashes; very dark eyebrows; a long bony nose, slightly twisted towards the left; a square, short moustache like a little black patch; instead of the mouth, a slit from ear to ear, and the ears were a pair of felt slippers hanging from both sides of the skull, and the skull was a polished bowling-ball, with bits of hair plastered down any-which-way and cobbled with scabs.

He was dressed in a silk gown the colour of red wine, down to the knees, and around his neck he had draped a cravat made out of the same material. When Coral Queen had him within her reach, she was invaded by the perfume the man gave off like an aura, a sombre and ecclesiastical scent that she associated, without asking why, with top government administrators, ministers or chiefs of police. The man, hands in the pockets of his dressing-gown, was scrutinizing his visitor with those hard-boiled eyes that seemed not to see but that saw everything. The slit of the mouth began to open little by little like a badly sewn wound, he smiled a difficult smile, either of approval or of apology for not having smiled before. He pretended to take a small gift out of his pocket and what he took out was his hand, which he extended cautiously, as if he were offering her a precious and fragile object and was afraid that this woman, so hefty, would damage it. (When Coral Queen shook it, she had the impression of holding a piece of ivory, so smooth, hard and cold was his hand.) And finally he spoke. The truth is that Coral Queen had not expected someone so physically disadvantaged to bring forth such a subterranean voice.

'I'm very grateful to you for having come.'

But the tone made the words say exactly the contrary: that it was she who should be grateful for having been invited. So she mumbled:

'Thank you very much.'

As if displeased by the fact that Coral Queen had seized his subtle innuendo, the man withdrew the hand brusquely, made it fly with an imperious gesture and waved it towards the forest of furniture.

'Please take a seat.'

She walked towards the luxurious objects that stood as if waiting to attack her, saw an empty armchair, and sat down, but with barely a segment of her buttocks. In the meantime, the man walked up to a table laden with bottles and glasses. There, with the impeccable gestures of a salesman in the presence of a client, he placed a finger on each of the bottles in turn.

'What can I offer you? A cognac? A liqueur? Or would you rather have a sherry?'

On an empty stomach it will make me sick, she thought.

'A cognac, if it's not too much trouble.'

She took advantage of the fact that he had his back turned towards her (a tiny narrow back from which the shoulder-blades stuck out like the panes of a half-open window) to steal a quick ocular inspection of the room. The man might be ugly and have an insignificant body, but no one could have said he wasn't rich. In that room alone there were so many costly things that if one sold them or pawned them they would allow one to live in luxury for at least five hundred years. She spotted the clock, large-bellied and golden, on the mantelpiece, between two monstrous pieces of china.

He approached her with a glass in each hand (and Coral Queen, putting an end to the inspection, drew her eyes up to the silk knot that clasped the boyish waist), offered one to his guest and then sank down into a coffee-coloured tub, crossed his legs (with one glance she made a mental inventory of his black trousers with narrow cuffs, the black socks, the black boots with military heels, funereal accoutrements of a uniform the little man no doubt wore under the silk gown and which brought to mind a disciplinary profession), crossed the legs, as I was saying, with obvious delight, as if crossing them were his favourite occupation, looked at his glass, made it swivel in his hands, and coughed out:

'Really, I'm most grateful.'

But in another tone of voice, a tone that corrected the previous statement or refuted Coral Queen's perspicacity.

Finally, as if to bring the misunderstanding to an end, he took a sip of his cognac. She felt exhorted to follow suit. The cognac was bitter and strong. *I'll get drunk,* she thought.

The little man was swinging one leg over the other. With his left hand he held his glass, with his right one he fingered the moustache patch to keep it in place. The bulging eyes scrutinized the entire room as if to make certain that nothing was missing. Coral Queen, instead, was watching him. She was asking herself how it was possible that such a puny little man could give this impression of being powerful and even fearful. It wasn't only the luxury that surrounded him and belonged to him. It was something else that came from the man himself. Perhaps a long-standing habit of giving orders and being obeyed. Perhaps his government post, his job at the police. Or perhaps the sensation that, beneath his dismantled appearance, he hid an irascible character. Perhaps all rich people, even the weaklings, give an impression of being powerful and of provoking fear.

To sum things up: if the looks of the owner of the house seemed to Coral Queen unworthy of the decor,

the intimidating atmosphere that surrounded her suf-
ficed to convince her that among the Powers That Be
remarkable bodies are unnecessary. Money is all that
matters. Therefore the respect and fear she felt for the
little man didn't vanish. But there was something curious: she no longer asked herself why she had come. It
seemed to her that the mystery had been solved. Now
all she had to do was wait for him to speak. In some
uncanny way she felt herself to be ready. And the man's
behaviour intimated that everything had been planned
for her own good.

The man began by dropping his priestly airs.

'Willy tells me that you perform a very interesting
act, very exotic. Willy is the young man who brought
you here in the car.'

And when did he tell you that? Coral Queen thought to
herself. As if reading her mind, the man explained:

'Last week he went to the theatre. He returned full
of enthusiasm for you.'

'Very kind of him.'

'He told me that your act is the best of the show.'

'Many thanks.'

'Something that one doesn't often see in Buenos
Aires.'

He spoke without looking at her. He kept staring at
the walls, at the books, at the knick-knacks. Two possi-
bilities: either he had been disappointed by Coral

Queen's looks and had no wish to persist, or he had been so fully satisfied that he felt no need to undertake a second inspection. Or perhaps between a man like himself and a woman like Coral Queen, it was his prerogative to be admired whatever his ugliness, and her obligation to study him as if he were a fashion model.

Whatever the case might be, the fact is that he was behaving just like a young lady admitting an admirer into her bedchamber. To prevent him from imagining that she's a loose woman, or to keep him at bay until she sees fit, the young lady converses with her beau but without looking at him, always casting her eyes sideways, so that the forward gentleman understands that she is not inciting him to anything and that if he decides to take the initiative, he—and he alone—will be to blame.

'Have you been working long in that theatre?'

'Not long. Three years.'

'And where were you performing before?'

'At the Argentina.'

'What is that?'

'Another theatre, not far from the Cosmopolitan.'

'And is it true that you are from the Caribbean?'

'Those are the manager's inventions.'

'I thought as much. I imagine that neither are you a cannibal.'

And without opening the scar that was a mouth he

excreted a picaresque cackle that Coral Queen dared not imitate. In an atmosphere like this one, only those who feel at home are entitled to laugh.

'Thank God,' she said haughtily, as if defending herself from slander.

'But the stage name has lent you success.'

'I can't complain.'

'I imagine you must have many admirers.'

'Well, you know, admirers are never lacking.'

'I know, I know.'

But Coral Queen wasn't following the rules of the young lady's game with the beau in the boudoir. Determined to make a good impression, she persevered in the manners of the matron receiving condolences, sitting up straight in the armchair with only the tip of the coccyx touching the seat, not even drinking the cognac so as not to make herself giddy and lose her composure, holding the glass like someone holding someone else's chamber-pot, and when she spoke she constructed for herself an unctuous voice like that of a mother superior chatting with a bishop before entering together the confessional.

The man, as far as he was concerned, proceeded with the useless flirtations. The little leg kept swinging back and forth, the bulging eyes kept roaming through the room, now the free hand dangled in the air to show off the manicured nails and the gold ring on the little finger (but it wasn't, like that of the Russkies, a square and groping hand, rather a delicate hand, in spite of the veins sculpted in relief). Every so often he'd take a sip of cognac to lend himself courage.

'City hall, the police, don't bother you?'

'Bother me?'

'I ask only because in this country we have such hypocritical morals.'

'No bothers.'

'I'm glad. In Europe things are so different. Have you ever been to Europe?'

'Not yet.'

'In Paris, for instance, you'd be a famous *vedette*. I'm not saying you're not one here. But if you were working in Paris, your name would be on everyone's lips.'

'Do you really think so?'

'But of course. In France I've seen many similar shows, and I can assure you they're very successful. Naturally, there's another class of people there, other customs, another mentality. Willy told me that the Cosmopolitan's public is not very well-behaved, to say the least.'

'They come in all sizes.'

'I imagine. He also told me that with you it's different, with you the public behaves properly and gives you a resounding applause.'

'Well, yes.'

'So in fact, you deserve something better than the Cosmopolitan.'

For Coral Queen, all her suppositions flared up again, one after the other. The man wanted to get her between the sheets. He had sent the blond after her because a gentleman of his class doesn't deign to set foot in the poorer neighbourhoods. The man was too puffed up to have any kind of personal interest in the women of Veinticinco de Mayo. The man would offer her a contract and take her with him to Paris, where chorus girls like herself were so incredibly successful. The man was the stranger who was to change her life.

She had no time to think further because at that very moment the prim young lady realized that the beau in her bedroom was more than a bit of a fool and was not going to impinge on her coyness. It was time for him to make a decision: either he attacked her or he left. So he uncrossed his sticks and abandoned his glass on a table, and stood up and began to walk about. One hand on the slender waist, the other tucked inside the cravat, he walked with the swagger of a schoolgirl showing off her new clothes to the visitors. All of a sudden, the gritty voice softened with insinuating intonations and the commanding ring broke down into mischievous or flirtatious tinklings.

'You know what it is about you that I like so much? That you behave with such impeccable correctness.

Because some imbecile might think that you, off stage, might be, I don't know how to say this, you know what I mean. But you're not, and I like that very much. Very much indeed.'

He repeated that 'very much' with such vehemence that his deep voice became suddenly effeminate. Coral Queen realized with admiration that the man regarded her as a very decent woman, a lady capable of entering palaces and mansions without anyone barring her path. To confirm that opinion and to earn further merits, she became almost lugubrious in her severity.

'There are those who think poorly of us artists, but they're wrong.'

The man became impassioned:

'Those are people with stupid prejudices. Don't pay any attention to them. Morons who still live in the age of cavemen. That's not how it is in Europe. In Europe artists are received in the finest homes, and with all honours. But here we continue to live like backward puritans.'

And suddenly he changed the subject.

'What's your name?'

Coral Queen thought it was someone else who had spoken. But it had been the man himself, all of a sudden wary, to judge by the faint little voice and the shiver that passed through the whole length of the wine-coloured dressing-gown. Once again, his hands were in his pockets, and it was probably those very same hands that were trembling.

Somewhat slow to follow the somersaults of the conversation, she asked:

'Who? Me?'

The man, who had stopped to look at her, started walking again with his eyes glued to the carpet. He seemed hunched up, holding his underbelly with both his hands. Something was undermining his authoritarian airs. Something, something that he feared or felt ashamed of.

'I know your stage name is Coral Queen,' and his voice got caught in a fake little cough. 'But I'd like to know your real name. If you don't think it indiscreet of me to ask.'

He said it as if he were asking her what her fee was, a thorny subject that someone of his rank had difficulty in broaching.

And then Coral Queen understood. She understood that she was at the gates of a revelation that would change her life, but that the key to those gates depended on whether she had a certain name and no other, because under any other name the gates would remain locked forever. That was why the man had been proceeding with such finicky circumspection.

She was in a panic. She was in a panic that her name might not fit in the lock, and that the Englishman's labours, the car ride, the niceties of the gentleman, cognac included, might result in nothing but a useless waste. The man's bile would rise. *He'll send me to jail,* she thought. She was unable to utter a single sound. She didn't dare pronounce that name that was a passport to heaven or hell. All she did was stare at the diminutive Saint Peter. Stare at him and gulp.

He continued to walk about with sunken shoulders and the hands on his underbelly as if to hold back the rage in his testicles. And yet, in spite of everything, before making a decision, he gave Coral Queen one last chance. He stopped next to the Cannibal Woman, stared at the wall and gurgled with asthmatic wheezes:

'You'd rather not tell me? Why not? You'd rather I called you Coral Queen?'

She choked on her saliva and instead of speaking she uttered a sound reminiscent of drains.

He put an end to the questioning.

'All right then. After all, Coral Queen is a very pretty name.'

And as Coral Queen was saying to herself that the man was obviously offended even though he'd covered it up with that condescending compliment, and as Coral Queen was about to appease him by telling him her real name (and let whatever must happen, happen), as she was about to open her mouth and articulate the six syllables of her name, she saw with horror that the man was on the point of throwing himself at her, with the intention—she thought—of wringing her neck.

Not at all. He had fallen on his knees. He had knelt down and was clutching her in his wicker arms, kissing her neck, leaking hungry baby wailings, sobs, shivering in agony or in heat. It all happened so quickly that Coral Queen had only time to see the melted dribblings running down his scabby skull, to feel against her flesh that damp and feverish mask, the pointed nose that probed her like a modest and semi-erect member, the split mouth oozing gobs of spittle. The ecclesiastical scent was growing sulphurous as it mingled with the odours of the armpits. Cramps ran up and down the brittle arms.

She lowered her eyes and saw the emaciated body, the miserable curves of the thighs covered by the silk, the ankles encased in crumpled trouser legs, the crooked socks, the showy military heels. She remembered the Russkies. She thought that this mannikin was a variant of the Russkies, with better manners, and worse endowed by Nature. She felt repulsion, fatigue. Then she thought that the poor mannikin forgave her the name and that all that show stemmed from too great an illusion and the fear of losing her. Always inclined to be grateful, she patted the shrivelled neck with one hand while with the other she balanced the glass that threatened to spill the cognac.

Feeling the caress on the neck, the little man grew bolder. He began to whine promises like a punished child who tries not to be left without dessert.

'Coral Queen! My Queen! Stay here and live with me! You'll live like a queen! I'll buy you jewellery, furs, gowns, anything you wish! You'll be my woman! My wife!'

And he seemed to dissolve completely into spittle.

Coral Queen gasped for breath. Not as much because of the whiner's attack, but because of that other weight, the weight of unbelievable bliss. Tatters, I mean less than tatters, frayed threads of thoughts became entangled inside her head. Loose words appeared and disappeared, sentences cut in half like earthworms, each half alive and thrashing. His woman. His wife. With or without a marriage licence, his wife. Furs, jewels, gowns. The whole mansion with all its knick-knacks. The garden, the statue, the iron gates, the car, the neighbourhood of palatial houses, the world of the rich. She, the Cannibal Woman of the Cosmopolitan, all of a sudden, from one day to the next, bang, a *grande dame,* a lady, the wife of a government official, the minister's wife, the wife of the chief of police. And maybe, when the mannikin was all spent, it would be Willy's turn. No, not that. A chorus girl might do that, but not a lady. One should always be grateful. Even if the mannikin were unable to function, she'd be faithful. His woman. Like a queen. Rides in the car, maybe a trip to Europe. Furs, jewels, gowns. She was choking, she'd have wanted to tear off the little man with his bothersome libido, this wasn't the time for gropings. She needed to stand up, to walk about. Was she dreaming? Wasn't there in all this some terrible mistake? And if after all this, the affair concerned not her but someone else? First the honey, then the gall. No, best to clear things up now, just in case. You don't trifle with the rich. They make you pay dearly for any mistake, even if it's theirs. Best to tell him her name.

'My name is Arabia Badur.'

And in the meantime she prayed God that there should be no mistake.

Instantly the little man stopped his slavering. He drew back, opened his arms, looked sideways. He remained on his knees, but now he was trying to place the source of a sound, a small distant voice that had forced him to stop his struggles with Coral Queen. And all her enthusiasm disappeared down the gutter.

Nevertheless she repeated, with a voice now rather sickly:

'My real name is Arabia Badur.'

He rose to his feet, took a few random steps, found a huge piece of furniture in his way and came to a halt. He was still trying to find the source of the sound, of the remote voice.

Coral Queen felt a different type of terror. The terror of having spoken too late, that this was perhaps a more serious mistake than having spoken too soon. Now the little man would not forgive her having allowed him to fall on his knees in front of her as if she'd been a saint standing on an altar. He would not forgive her the spurting of his libido, the releasing of all those promises of living together, of buying her furs and jewels, of treating her like a queen.

She reasoned that it might be best to insist, so that he might see, in time or too late, that she had not meant to deceive him.

'Truly, my name is Arabia Badur.'

The man turned towards her but didn't look at her. From the corner of his eyes he was glancing at the bunch of tea roses. He was no longer the punished child who barely a moment ago was begging not to be punished. He was now, once again, the fearful and powerful person, aged by another ten years. The ardour of the struggle had wilted the starch of his face and the assorted features threatened to come unstuck. Even his nose had turned pale. Suddenly he was an old man whose age-masking devices had been slapped clear off his face. Even his silk gown changed into a ridiculous female dress that the old man wore as a costume and which was several sizes too big for him. And the cravat round his neck was an untidy scarf protecting him from chronic bronchitis.

What was he doing, in the meantime? He was staring at the tea roses. He seemed to be learning by heart the name Coral Queen had pronounced, repeating it to himself. Yes, that was it, because then he said it again, with a flutter of both lips of the gash. And finally he asked:

'Arabia Badur? You're not lying to me?'

A spark lit Coral Queen's mind. She thought she understood. The man had thought it impossible that her name was Arabia Badur. He had doubts, the miscreant. He wanted to be sure, as if the name Arabia Badur were a surplus of good luck.

Coral Queen opened her huge purse, stirred its chaotic interior, sought and found her I.D. card, opened it up for him to see on the page where it was written that she wasn't lying even though the photograph was that of a young girl with the face of someone mentally retarded.

But he remained motionless, adamant in his wary hesitations that he seemed to be submitting for an opinion to the tea roses.

'Look,' said Coral Queen. 'Here's my I.D.'

First he hid his hands inside the pockets of his gown, as if refusing to sully them with that document. Then he agreed to glance at it over his shoulder, which he lowered in order to see more clearly. Then he leaned over the paper and spelled out one by one the official statements confirming that the Cannibal Woman's name was Arabia Badur, daughter of father unknown and of Zulema Badur, born in Loreto, in the Province of Santiago del Estero, no distinctive birthmarks. Then he straightened himself up and shot a reproving glance at Coral Queen, while all his features broke into shivers of anger, repulsion and scorn. Then he looked away as if confronted with an indecorous sight. And finally he walked to the door, opened it and stepped out never to return.

Coral Queen heard the shouts immediately, the old man's voice crying out:

'You idiot! What did you bring me? She's a woman, you fool! She's a woman!'

When the cabin-boy, Willy, appeared on the threshold, she was already leaving the room. She stopped in front of him and looked him in the eye. They looked at one another, because he too fixed his eyes on her. Coral Queen had stopped to spit into his face the muck of some filthy word. But immediately she changed her mind. The young man was still chewing candy. He was still enveloped in that quiet and self-assured strength. Only that now he was no longer an angel but a demon. Without making a dent in his impassive armour, without interrupting the chewing of the candy, he seemed fully capable of giving her a beating if she as much as appeared to show signs of insubordination. No denying it, she was afraid. Therefore, swallowing her spittle, she walked out in front of him and towards the stairs. Halfway down he overtook her and now was in the lead.

They crossed the two halls, the antechamber. Once again Coral Queen refrained from lifting her eyes from the successive carpets. Not because she felt ashamed now, at least not the same kind of shame. That house wasn't the decor for a life as beautiful as a beautiful play. It was a decor filthier than that of the Cosmopolitan, except that it was more luxurious. It was a contrived Cosmopolitan where sick old men played out, for no public at all, the muck of their depravity. She even thought she felt in her nostrils the itch of something rotting. She couldn't wait to leave this last room.

When they reached the door, the blond man stepped aside to let her pass. She noticed on his face the terrible glimmer of the mercury eyes, and once again was afraid that the false angel would punish her. She hurried out. They crossed the garden. Now the footsteps on the brick-dust path sounded like a succession of rips in an old tarpaulin. The gates looked like those of a prison. And beyond, the darkness of night was like a total emptiness, like nothing.

The young man climbed into the car, started the engine, switched on the headlights. But Coral Queen was already escaping down the sidewalk. With her long legs she ran lifting spirals of leaves softened by the dew.

At the corner she took a side-street. She kept running, on tiptoe. She ran one block or two or who knows how many. The beads of sweat that kept rolling down under her clothes and the violent bellowing of her heart forced her to stop the race. At any rate, she was advancing fast. Now she hit the pavement and the piles of leaves with strong taps of her heels.

The street she was on was a tunnel identical to the previous one: the same serviceable lightbulbs cocooned in the same grimy wrappings, the same dome with its same arabesques, the same cobbles shining mistily like puddles of brackish water. On either side, one after the other, were rows of hedges, spear-tipped fences, garden gates and behind, the gardens and the lugubrious palaces with their votive lamps watching over their dreams of vice, morbidity, madness, death. From above, slow drips of gob fell upon her, spat with the veiled wrath with which the neighbourhood chased away the intruder. A mist or rather a fogged-up atmosphere effaced all outlines. The neighbourhood was a vast and cloying outhouse.

She fancied that the tunnel was drilling through the night as she advanced, but that it lead her nowhere. At another corner she turned again. Then again. She was under the impression that she was being met always by the same street with the same hedges and the same mounds heaped in the same gardens. *I'm going round in circles,* she thought. To escape from that maze she walked back half a block and took off in the opposite direction.

A few steps away a sort of barrier blocked the street. On the other side she could see a large open space and further ahead a row of lights. She came nearer and looked. She saw the tracks, glittering among the grass like long needles. She saw the signal-tower with two green welcoming eyes. She saw, on the other side of the tracks, a neighbourhood of white houses all identical. And at the far end a lit-up avenue through which, at that very moment, a decent streetcar was passing.

At one end of the barrier was a turnstile. She went through it and crossed over a bridge made out of planks.

And right then and there she felt what even up to this very day she imagines was a grace of God who now at last had decided to look upon her and protect her. She felt that crossing the railroad tracks was not taking place in space but in time. That it was like passing from one time to another, from one age to another age. It was like leaving that which had already happened and entering that which was about to happen. Behind her was a memory of foul events; in front, no memory but hope. Behind, the years as the Cannibal Woman were fading into nothing, together with the whole lot of chorus girls, dancers, spectators, managers, Russkies, old men hidden in a vast mansion waiting for a transvestite, and ruffians disguised as English tourists.

In front lay the years of Arabia Badur, resurrected after a long sleep that had lasted since her arrival in Buenos Aires, and she felt as willing as she had felt then to earn an honest living. When she finished crossing the tracks, an explosion of vertiginous lights split in two forever the story of this woman walking away down a clear little street.

She had only a small amount of money in her purse. She had no other clothes than those which she was wearing. She had no trade. But if Zulema Badur, illiterate and all, burdened with age and children, had been able to survive, so would Arabia. And this neighbourhood seemed to her far, far better than the place from which she'd come so many years ago.

AFTERWORD

For years he sold insurance, and something of the archetypical insurance salesman has stuck to his appearance: the polished face, the attentive look, the trimmed moustache, the constant suit—even though he 'walked away from that office desk for the last time on September 30 1968, at eight p.m. precisely, to be nothing but a writer.' While still at the office, 'shuffling papers with great efficiency,' he wrote his first novel, *Rose at Ten,* a brilliant mystery (miserably translated into English a few years later) that won him in 1955, at the age of thirty-three, the important Kraft Publishers Prize for Fiction. After the success of the novel, Denevi turned to the theatre: *The Official Files* and *The Emperor of China* were produced in quick succession. Then, in 1960, Denevi's short story 'Secret Ceremony' won the *Life in Spanish* Prize, selected among 3,149 entries by a jury presided over by Octavio Paz. (Once again, the English-speaking public was betrayed by Denevi's interpreters: this time by the British filmmaker Joseph Losey who turned the superb story into a muddled melodrama with Mia Farrow,

Elizabeth Taylor and the unnecessary Robert Mitchum.)

Denevi doesn't like to travel. He lives alone in a small house in one of the quieter neighbourhoods of Buenos Aires, writing in the mornings and playing tangos on the piano in the afternoons. 'I have my disciplines,' he says. 'To write every day (even if what I write won't get published); to write the finished thing, not drafts (even if I have to rewrite the same page ten times); to write during the day (but collect my material at night); to write on the typewriter (so that my writing has from its very beginning the character of the printed page); before writing, to read a good book for half an hour (to create the right atmosphere; I find it impossible to go with no transition from the reading of the newspaper to the writing of a text that pretends to be literary).'

Denevi is, above all, a storyteller. His interest is in the plot, that neglected and snubbed core of fiction, but a plot told in an effusive and baroque language that draws from eighteenth- and nineteenth-century Spanish, a language that, in Denevi, is never arch or pompous, but rich and comic and precise. In that 'multitudinous Spanish' (as he calls it) he has written several more novels, plays, a collection of social commentary and his unsettling tales.

Three of the four stories in this volume are drawn

from two collections: *Hierba del cielo* (1973) and *Reunión de desaparecidos* (1977); 'Eine kleine Nachtmusik' was never published in book form in Spanish.

Alberto Manguel, Sélestat, April 1993